# ANNE *of the* FENS

# ANNE *of the* FENS

From the Bradstreet Chronicles

Gretchen Gibbs

GLENMERE PRESS · WARWICK, NEW YORK

Library of Congress Control Number: 2015935379
Glenmere Press, Warwick, NY
ISBN 978-0-9852948-8-5

Photographs by Diane Pell Photographer and Stephen Almond Photography
Cover design by Robin Ludwig Design Inc.

GLENMERE PRESS
WARWICK, NEW YORK

# ANNE *of the* FENS

# CHAPTER ONE

*May 1627 – Lincolnshire, England, town of Boston*

I LOOKED AROUND and saw a splash of green disappearing around the dark corner of the church, in the direction of the market square.

"I'll catch her," I shouted to the rest of my family as they filed into St. Botolph's.

Confound my little sister! I ran after her, wishing I were not dressed for Sunday services in a skirt that stood out to make me twice my usual width. I was nearing the corner of our huge church when I stubbed my toe on the cobblestones. I swore under my breath then hurried on, Sarah lost to sight.

Last night, Father had carried on at dinner, calling the May Fair a sinful nest of rogues and scalliwags who dishonored the holy day, stuffed their faces with roasted meats and sweets, listened to lewd plays, picked pockets, and assaulted young women.

I knew that Sarah had heard nothing about the dangers, only the sweets. I would find her at the booths that sold anything sugared. How did I know her so well? Mother had chosen the right person to mind her—I cared nothing about the confections, but I wanted to see the dancing and the plays. I wanted to see the young men. How would they look at me in my beautiful blue Sunday gown? The only men I got to see were in church, dressed in black and thinking holy thoughts. I wished I could keep my own thoughts more holy.

I ROUNDED THE corner and stopped in horror, choking from the smell of people, sheep, horses, goats, pigs, cattle and chickens. The square was packed so full that nothing could move. I could not see Sarah nor push into the fair at all. There were hundreds of sheep in front of me, and I kicked one in frustration. It bleated, moving only a little. Sarah, smaller than I, would be trampled if she tried to move among them.

I would have to force my way through the flock and hope I would not encounter their owner. It was at least safer than trying to get through crowds of men who might attack me.

As I neared the last of the sheep, a whirl of greasy smoke signaled the meat vendors. Perhaps the sweet stands were nearby. It was the barley sugar drops that would call to Sarah. I found the meat vendor, where men stood about gnawing on huge ribs of beef or turkey drumsticks. I could spy barley sugar in the next stand, and swarms of people, but no Sarah. Had she made her purchase and gone? I pushed to the front of the line, in spite of the curses thrown at me, and shouted at the vendor, had he seen a young girl in a green dress? He acted as though he hadn't heard me. His face was covered with horrid pock marks, and I shuddered as I turned away.

Had someone picked up Sarah for a ransom? Her clothes would show that her family had a little money. I was out of breath from the pushing and pummeling of the crowd, but at the thought that she was gone I felt weak, and my breath came truly fast.

Which way to go?

I heard music and found myself moving toward it with the

crowd. Several couples danced wildly. As I stood there, a young man grabbed me by the waist, pulling me toward him. He was handsome, with blond curly hair and a bold eye. I could smell beer on his breath and the perspiration that stained his red tunic.

"Dance with me, wench," he said.

My skin tingled where he touched me. I shut my eyes as he twirled me, and blood rushed to my head. It was what I had imagined. What I had wanted. But it was happening so fast. I felt a pang of fear when he pulled me closer, his body warm against me, and I kicked him, aiming for his shins.

He yelled in pain and let me go. "You common-kissing harpy!"

Shaking, I forced myself into the crowd again, looking wildly about. It was then I heard a woman's voice raised in anguish.

"Wherefore art thou, Romeo?"

I turned to see a young woman upon a stage, hands clasped to her heart. I stopped, knowing I must hear more. She called for her lover, and he answered.

People shoved at me and stepped on my feet, but I did not feel it. I forgot about Sarah, I forgot about my family in the church, I watched on. The lovers' families despised one another, but Romeo and Juliet intended to overcome their hatred. They might be forced to say good night, but they were determined to marry.

"Parting is such sweet sorrow." Romeo's voice was loving as he reached up to the balcony for her hand.

A sharp jab in my side brought me out of my spell. There was Sarah, icing dripping down her chin. I wanted to hug her and shake her at the same time.

"Ha, ha, found you out! Wait till I tell Father you watched the heathen play!" she said.

"Saucy urchin! Where have you been?"

But it was obvious from the icing where she had been. After the sweet stall she had found the cake stall, and I had missed her.

I grabbed her by the wrist and pulled her toward the gate. I led her back through the sheepfold, in spite of her protests that she was stepping in so many droppings that her shoes were in ruins. When I looked down I saw that my lovely blue skirt was covered with dust and grime.

At the edge of the sheepfold, a group of beggars stood. One, a large man in a rat-brown cloak, barred our way as we tried to pass out of the fair. Thin white hair fell over his forehead. He held his hand out toward us, as beggars do, and the open sore in his palm, crusted with pus, made me recoil.

"Do I offend you, Puritan gyle?" He had a Scottish accent.

I was both frightened at his blocking us and annoyed that he could tell so easily that I was a Puritan. I was not dowdy. My lace collar had eight inch points and my flaxen blue dress, however soiled, was in the latest fashion.

"Let us pass." I tried to sound firmer than I felt.

"A penny," he said with a leer.

"For what?"

"For my good will. For your good luck in coming out unhurt, two girls alone." He barred the way, and his body seemed menacing.

It was true that I had not seen other unescorted females in the fair. I reached into my pocket, found a couple of farthings, and put them into his disgusting palm. He looked at the tiny sum with contempt, but he gave way.

"I may see you again, Puritans," he shouted, as we ran on toward the church.

Sarah scolded me for giving him money. "I could have stomped on his foot, and we could have run past him."

"There were other beggars there, probably his friends."

She continued to cross me. "You didn't find me, you know, I found you. I was going back when I saw a gaping buffoon watching the play."

4

In the market we passed the notice board and we both stopped to look, though Sarah was not a good reader. The board was an important source of information about what was happening, and everybody read it regularly. I recognized a notice urging people not to pay the King's tax, a notice I had seen before. Sarah asked what it said, and when I told her, she asked why someone would have posted it.

"To get more people to know that he thinks the King is a bad man," I said, trying to explain it in terms she would understand.

Satisfied, she looked up at me with a crafty smile. "I won't tell about the fair if you don't."

I was torn. I should not let her get the better of me. However, if I told, Father would be so angry, both at Sarah and me. Father had a temper, and with all the conflict going on now in England, he seemed to explode even more than usual. The whole family would suffer for days.

No real harm had come to either of us, although Mother would despair over our clothing. In the end, I wiped Sarah's chin with my handkerchief and told her I would not tell if she promised never to do such a thing again.

She swore by all that is holy, but there was a smile on her face, and I did not believe her.

## CHAPTER TWO

WE STOLE INTO the back of the church and stood among the common folk. Mother was sitting on a bench in the front, craning her neck around. When she finally saw us, we waved calmly as though we had been there a long time. Reverend Cotton went on preaching, low and earnest, from his dark cherry pulpit.

His theme was *Render unto Caesar what is Caesar's and unto God what is God's*. He asked, however, *What if Caesar's will is contrary to God's will?* Even I, even Sarah, knew that he was talking about the King imposing a tax to fight his war in Spain. I had paid little attention to the matter, though I knew we had moved back to Tattershall Castle from our house here in the city of Boston because of it. Boston was not a big city, not like London, but Mother liked the hustle and bustle.

The sermon went on for hours, and it was especially hard to listen because of having to stand. I shifted my weight from foot to foot and thought about the fair, the dance music, and the words in the play. The young man with the blond curls and the bright red tunic kept coming into my mind. He was the first man ever to have touched me. I could still feel the pressure of his fingers on my back. We would have twirled and twirled until I was dizzy. When he pulled me to him, it was like a lover's embrace, even if we were dancing. I felt weak just thinking about it.

I had begun reading my Bible when I was six years old. Why do I always have to be good? I almost spoke it aloud, and I wondered if I would be struck dead on the spot. Nothing happened.

Nobody understood. Patience, the prettiest of all of us four sisters, was more than a year younger. She was my friend as well as my sister, but she was too good to understand me. Sarah understood wickedness, but she was too young to understand the ways I wanted to be bad. I wanted to be held by a young man, to feel his arms about me, as I had in the dance. Kissing might be nice as well, but I did not know how that would feel.

Our Father who art in Heaven. I tried to say the Lord's Prayer over and over as a way of calming myself and forcing my feelings down—down deep into my toes where they would not bother me. I wanted to be held.

God would punish me. He had already punished me, with the illnesses I often suffered. I thought of the pock-marked man at the sweets stall at the fair and I shuddered again. If I did not stop these thoughts, I would probably get the pox. Did I have a fever? I would die in pain. I wanted to be held.

At last, Reverend Cotton was getting louder and waving his arms, meaning he was coming to the end. After he and the rest of the congregation filed out, Sarah and I found the rest of the family. Father was talking to Simon, his assistant and my tutor, and some other friends.

"Masterful, how he manages to avoid being arrested for treason, or at least being removed as minister," Simon said.

Father was so taken with the sermon that he forgot about Sarah escaping into the fair. But when Simon left for his horse that would take him back to the castle, and the rest of us started to climb into the carriage, Father turned to Sarah and roared, "You hare-brained minnow, where did you go?"

Sarah quickly said that she had seen a cat that was just like Josie, who had left home and not returned. The cat had run into the fair and she had chased her. Then she was caught among all the people and could not move. I said that I, too, had become caught in the crowd, and we had only found each other by chance. I prayed to God to forgive my lie. Father looked at us suspiciously.

"You didn't set out to see the fair?"

"Oh no, Father," Sarah said.

Father pulled himself up to the top of the carriage with the coachman, and we were all relieved. I wished I could lie as well as Sarah, and then I wished that I were a better person, not so much like Sarah.

We helped Mother into the best seat in the carriage, facing forward on the outside, where there was less dust. Baby Mercy jumped in next, sitting close to Mother. We shouldn't have called Mercy a baby, as she was seven, just a year younger than Sarah, but the name stuck because she acted like a baby, and Mother spoiled her. Mercy lisped.

That left Sarah and me and Patience, my sister closest in age, for the other side of the carriage, facing backwards. In the carriage we rocked and jogged along, eating a lunch of bread and hard cheese. Father was proud of our carriage with its two horses and its wide seats and small windows. It was not as fancy as the Earl's, which had leather seats, but it carried the whole family and it was handsome. The Earl often came to services in Boston with his family, in the big carriage with the gold decorations, but he had not come today.

Mother sighed, "If only we were going back to our house…" Mother loved our house in Boston, and hated living in the castle. This was a difficult time in England, and Father needed to help the Earl, who was quite a young man. We were missing afternoon services because it would take hours to travel the twelve miles back to Tattershall Castle. I said nothing, but secretly I loved that we were living in the castle.

There was a great deal that I did not say to others. As during the sermon that morning, thoughts of Romeo and Juliet and the young man in the red tunic began to swirl through my mind. The wooden bench was hard, and Sarah's elbow poked into my side.

Finally I fell asleep, the wheels of the carriage seeming to say, "to be held, to be held, to be held."


I WOKE UP at a sharp pain on my ankle. I started to slap at it then realized it was a flea. I had a special way of killing fleas, rolling them between my fingers till they were stunned and then pressing them between my fingernails. Catching them was the hard part.

Sarah and I were probably covered with fleas from wading through the sheep. I looked over at Sarah, who was gazing out the window. Tiny black specks hopped against the white of her collar.

Patience was asleep in one corner, her dark hair peeping out of her bonnet, and Mother was asleep in the corner on the other side. Baby Mercy was leaning on Mother and pulling at her arm. "Mother, Tharah kicked me!"

I followed Sarah's gaze out the window, at the wide fens with their high grasses. It was good to see them green, after the dead winter.

Mother woke and chastised Sarah. We crossed the moat to the castle just then. The drawbridge was down, as it usually is, and Eric, the guard, let us through without stopping us.

It was late in the afternoon, the sky overcast and damp, when we got out of the carriage.

Mother muttered about our lodgings on the third floor, as she always did. I heard something about huge cold rooms, dampness, and the uneven stairs.

Before we had left for the castle this spring, I overheard a conversation between her and Father.

"You are my wife, no?"

I did not hear her reply.

"Then you cannot live twelve miles away from me."

That was one argument I was glad Father had won, as we would have stayed with Mother if she had remained in Boston.

USUALLY I DID not mind the stairs, but tonight I was coughing and out of breath by the time we reached the third floor. Patience and I headed to the room we shared off the main hall. It was a small room on the south side of the castle. We liked that the sun came in Early to wake us each morning, if only from a small slit of a window.

The room had no necessary. I did not like the smell of the rooms with necessaries, as the waste went down the channel in the castle wall to the ground or into the moat, and the room smelled. On the third floor the smell was less than lower down in the castle. I think that was why the Earl and his family lived on the fourth floor.

We began getting undressed for bed. I first took off the waistcoat I wore over my shift, the long shirt that we wore at all times, then the stomacher, the stuffed band of fabric we wore right below the waist to keep our skirts flaring out, and then the skirts themselves. I sighed over my blue skirt; it would take some poor laundress hours to get out the stains.

Patience took off her white, starched bonnet with care, putting it on its stand. She sighed.

"What?"

"Only thinking of my ears." Patience believes that her ears are too large and that they stick out. She worries that when she marries and has to take off her bonnet on the first night, her husband, appalled, will want to call the whole thing off. Sarah calls her Rabbit, or Elephant.

"Stop it. They are fine. What if you were one of the Puritan martyrs who had their ears cut off? Now that would be ugly."

"What a mean thing to say!"

It was, and I apologized. I had spoken from jealousy. Patience was beautiful, with pale skin, long dark hair, and gray-green eyes. I wished I could look like her. My own hair was brown with a reddish tint, straight like Patience's but unkempt, and I, like Patience, was glad to wear a bonnet, although we were hiding different things. I had freckles and, every now and then, a small blemish on my chin. My nose was too large, and my eyes sometimes had an unfocused look, because my vision was bad and things became blurry. Patience sometimes said my eyes were one of my good features, and that they were luminous. I was not quite sure what that meant, but it sounded nice. She also has said that, when I smiled, I became beautiful.

When I looked in Mother's Venetian mirror, I was so disappointed at the face that stared back at me. I would not want that person as a friend. Then I tried smiling, and it was not so bad.

There were more interesting things to talk about than our looks. As we got into bed, I told Patience what had happened, about chasing Sarah, the man who danced with me, and about the play—as much of the story as I had heard. The more I told her, the more I wanted to know the ending.

"What do you think might have happened at the friar's when they went to get married?" I asked.

Patience's body went stiff beside me in the bed.

"I do not know, but I know it is a sin for women to display themselves in a public play."

I said she knew that the part was probably played by a young man, but she said nothing and turned away from me in the bed.

"Someone in the crowd said it was by Shakespeare. By now I have looked at all the books in the library and there are none by Shakespeare. How do you think I can find the ending?" I ignored her crossness.

"I do not know, and if I did, God knows I should not help you."

Several minutes passed. Then Patience said, "I have heard Simon and Father speak of Shakespeare."

"What did they say?" I sat up.

"You are pulling the blankets off me."

I covered her with the blankets again, and she continued, "They said that the plays had humor if you overlooked the Godlessness."

I could get no more out of her. As I began to fall asleep, feeling slightly feverish, I was startled when Patience sat up in bed. Now it was I who had no blankets.

"Selfish Anne!" Her voice was loud. "All the problems we are facing and you want to read a heathen book about romance."

"What do you mean, the problems we are all facing?" I said sleepily. When Patience got very angry, it was usually after she had thought for a while.

"Did you listen to a word of the sermon today? Do you know how angry the King will be if the Earl and Father do not pay the tax?"

"But the King's war and the tax are unjust. He disbanded Parliament because he knew they would not vote for the tax. Nobody should pay the tax."

"The Earl and Father will be arrested and go to prison. We will have no father. Think about that for a while."

I had seldom seen Patience, who always saw the good in me, so angry. I patted her arm and said yes, I was a selfish, thoughtless girl and of course I did not want Father and the Earl to be arrested. But she was still angry.

# CHAPTER THREE

THE NEXT MORNING I was aware of Patience getting out of bed and slipping downstairs, the sun strong in the casement window. I woke again later to find her hovering over me and the sun already past the window. I groaned and turned over, every muscle in my body aching.

"Fen fever again," Patience said, without the anger of the previous night. She did not say what we were both thinking, that I was being punished for my selfish thoughts.

Where we live, many have fen fever, and some say it is due to the mosquitoes that swarm about the swampy ground. Once one gets the illness it is a part of life forever, bringing every few weeks or months a bout of high fever, trembling, and aching muscles. I find that, for me, it is brought on by fatigue. As I had chased Sarah into the fair and stood for hours in the church, I had worried that I would get sick.

Patience brought a wet cloth for my forehead and a flagon of beer for my thirst. She said that she would tell Mother I could not do chores, and she would tell Simon I would not come to the library for tutoring. The family was used to my illnesses.

Mother sent Marianne, the maid to the Earl's sister Arbella, to care for me. I loved talking to Marianne, as she knew all the gossip of the castle. She brought me wormwood in a tiny jar with a small wooden spoon. It tasted foul but it usually helped a bit with the aching. As I lay there, her long blond hair brushing over my face as she spooned medicine into me, something light struck me on the cheek. I looked down at a small wooden crucifix hanging from Marianne's neck. She saw it herself, jumped away, put the cross back inside her chemise, and turned a dull red.

"Marianne!"

"Are you going to tell?"

I did not answer.

She began to pace, head bowed over folded hands. Now that I knew it was there I could see the crucifix bouncing inside against her chemise. "Nobody knows. They would throw me out if they knew. I am a fine worker, I care for Arbella's things as though they were gold, I coddle her in every way—"

"I know." I smiled at her, and she stopped pacing.

Everyone knew Marianne worked hard. I asked her how she had deceived us, and she sat on the bed, took a breath, and began her story. She said that her father was a Puritan, which I had assumed, as he came to services regularly.

"Father fell in love with my mother and only found she was a Catholic later. He married her, regardless, as long as she told no one. When I was a child I came upon her praying with a crucifix. The more she told me about the Catholic faith, the more I wanted it for myself. She has taken me to secret services. The castle chapel and the church across the way—they are so bare. It honors God to show beautiful pictures and statues of Him, to have crosses and gold and song and splendor in a church."

The chapel in the castle and the village church across the way were as bare as any Puritan could want. The village church, which had been built near the castle some two hundred years before, was big, though four of its size would have fit into the Boston church we had attended yesterday, and it had probably contained statues and pictures and crosses, which Puritans destroyed. Now, the only color in the gray of stone was the windows. I did love to see the light coming through the ones in the south, staining the stone floors yellow and red.

"All that display distracts us from awareness of Him."

I had heard this so many times I said it without thought. But there was a niggling echo of her argument in my mind. "Splendor" was a lovely word.

"I won't give you away," I decided, "but you must tell me everything about the services."

"With pleasure."

She began to tell of priests dressed in robes of purple and gold with large gold crosses upon their chests, and velvet hats upon their heads, and the smell of incense in the air. I felt as I had at the fair, torn between the delights of the senses and knowing that such delights were sinful.

I wanted to know about confession.

"If you can gain forgiveness for all your sins, does that mean you can do whatever you want?

"No. You must repent, truly, in your heart, or God will not forgive you."

Marianne left soon after. I struggled out of bed and went to my little window. The sun was still shining sharp on the red brick of the castle walls. It was my earliest memory, the red brick of the castle glinting in the sun. Beauty. The play about Romeo and Juliet was beautiful. Beautiful things could be sinful but surely they did not have to be.

What to think about Catholicism?

Many people had taught me it was evil—Father, Mother, Simon, Reverend Cotton. Perhaps while the Catholic Church was evil, the people who practiced it were not all evil. Perhaps I could teach

Marianne. I realized it was she who had been teaching and I the one learning.

I returned to bed, shivering and sweating, and passed in and out of sleep. In my waking periods, I thought about religion and the play. Shakespeare was not a Catholic, but he was no Puritan. I think he had no religion, and lived in a Godless fashion. There had been lewd puns and rough humor in what I had heard at the fair.

The Earl had a wonderful library, containing hundreds of books. Not all of the books were by Puritan authors, but there were none that spoke against Puritanism.

I would certainly not be able to get back to the fair. To find the ending of the story, I needed to find the book. The only possibility was Simon, but could I manage to persuade him to tell me? And would he tell Father that I had asked?

# Chapter Four

The next day, when the light came through the window, I felt less achy and my forehead no longer burned. I rose with Patience and went with her to morning prayers in the chapel. How small and bare the chapel was, I thought. Four of its size could have fit into St. Botolph's, in Boston, where we attended services. After our breakfast of bread and milk, Mother said that I could spend the day in the library. One advantage of being sickly was that I had fewer chores and could spend more time reading and talking with Simon.

The castle had the same floor plan on each of its four floors, a huge central room, surrounded by smaller rooms, and small round rooms at the corners where the turrets were. The servants lived in the basement. The first floor, the grandest, was where the Earl entertained and held important events, like the wedding of his sister Arbella. The second floor held the chapel, Father's office where he heard complaints from the tenants of the estate, and the library in the large central room. We lived on the third, and the Earl's family lived on the top.

There were not enough books in the world to fill the second floor library entirely, but the whole north side of the room had shelves and shelves of books. There was a broad carved table of dark oak running halfway the width of the room facing the shelves, where Simon—my father's assistant and my tutor—was sitting that morning, his dark head poring over one thick volume, with others opened every which way around him.

"Greetings. Feeling better? You look pale as a dewberry."

I made a face at him. I had known Simon for four years, since I was eleven and he twenty, almost twice my age. He was handsome, tall, and well built, with wide shoulders and a narrow waist. He had fine, dark eyes.

In the past year or so, when I had started noticing men as men, I had thought of Simon in a different way. He was closer to my age now, it seemed, but he still acted only like a tutor.

Sometimes I tried to flirt a little, or wear something pretty when I was going to meet him, but he did not notice at all. He knew so much he was always interesting to talk with, though.

"How are the Punic Wars coming?" he asked me, motioning me to the short three-legged stool across the table from him.

I had been reading one of Father's favorite books, Raleigh's *History of the World*. Father said it had taken Raleigh fifteen years in prison to write it, and I could spend a few months on it. I had not finished the pages Simon had assigned me and I wanted to distract him. I also wanted to talk to him about what Marianne had told me, though I knew I had to be careful how I did it.

"Please, Simon, Mother says if we do not pay the King's tax we may be arrested. I think, then, we must pay it. What do you think?"

"It is an unlawful tax. The beetle-headed dwarf wants only to fund his war in Spain."

Simon always called King Charles a dwarf because he was so short, but over time his language had become more and more insulting.

"Could you be arrested for calling the King a beetle-headed dwarf?"

"Possibly. I trust you will not report me." Simon looked away, slightly embarrassed. I did not usually comment on his foul language toward the King.

"What if we are arrested?"

"Your father, the Earl, and I all believe we must act on our principles. Many, many are refusing to pay, and he cannot arrest us all. It is all because of his silly dream to marry the daughter of the Spanish King. He wants revenge for the rejection he received."

"Such a romantic story, like a fairy tale, King Charles crossing all of Europe in disguise to find and woo her." I knew I was making Simon angrier. His face was turning dark.

"Pah. Please, Anne. Don't be a silly, sentimental girl. Sometimes I think it is impossible to teach a girl."

I wanted to hit him but of course I could not.

He went on, "What if the King had agreed to her conditions? What if he had become Catholic? England could have burst into civil war."

"Is it so bad to be Catholic?" Now I could raise the question in my mind.

Simon stood up from the table and his voice was loud. "Anne, have you learned nothing from all my teaching, the Reverend Cotton's teaching, your father's teaching? What do you mean, is it so bad to be Catholic? You are a Puritan, pledged to purify the corrupt church. That should be the aim of everything we do. Is it so bad to be Catholic? God's teeth."

He went on, even louder. "Don't you remember our studies of the reign of Bloody Mary, before Elizabeth? How many Puritans did she kill?"

"At least three hundred."

"And how, may I ask?"

"Many of them were burned alive, in wicker baskets hung over flames."

My neck hurt from looking up at him, and I moved my stool back further from the table.

"I am not an idiot," I said, trying to sound dignified. "I know what it is to be a Puritan. I know what you are afraid of, that Charles will go back to Catholicism and then Puritans will be burned alive again. I am asking you something different. What I want to know is how about the person who is a Catholic. Is every Catholic a bad person? I don't think so."

"You have found a person who is Catholic and whom you like!" He scowled down at me. "Who is it?"

I blushed. Simon was so intelligent. I would have to be careful not to give Marianne away. I began to trace the grain of the wood in the oak table with my finger. I gathered my courage and looked up at him. "What if I have? Do you want to send her to the gallows? Is that how good Puritans act towards others? I certainly shall not tell you who it is."

He began to pace back and forth. "You are becoming impudent, young woman. Have you been listening to my conversations with your father?"

"No," I said honestly.

"I think we should try to convert Catholics and the King's Church of Englanders also. Your father feels that is impossible, and we might as well hang them or expel them. Or go somewhere we could leave them all behind."

"The New World?" I asked, feeling anxiety in my stomach.

"Perhaps," he said. "Or Holland."

I did not want to think about leaving my country. "I believe that this person is a good person."

Simon's dark eyebrows rose, and his eyes seemed bigger than ever, as he stopped pacing and looked into mine.

"You must tell me who it is."

"I shall not." I rose to my feet as well. "You don't trust me enough. I know what is good and bad in people." As I said it, I knew it was true. "You tutor me, but only to Puritan ideas. I want to read other things. I want to read Shakespeare." My voice was loud and shrill. I had meant to persuade Simon to help me find Shakespeare, not to challenge him like this.

"If you are so adult, then see if you can find Shakespeare. You will need the luck of the rabbit to do so." He looked at me hard, and I thought there was something significant about the rabbit. I knew that the servants said, "White rabbit, white rabbit, white rabbit," the first day of each month for luck. Did he mean that?

"What do you mean?"

"I have said too much already."

He was still angry, and so was I.

I LEFT THE room, breathing hard and a little red in the face myself. A silly, sentimental girl. Ha! Just because I was interested in men did not mean that I was silly or stupid. I climbed the circular stairs in the corner of the castle, up three flights to the roof. I thought of it as my place. Unless the Earl posted a guard because of some kind of danger, which hardly ever happened, I could be alone there.

The fens stretched away for miles in all directions. I could see the reeds and grasses close by, with the channels cut through them by men and nature. The distant view was flat as a rich green pancake, with some pieces of forest and farm lands sticking out. Watery places glimmered in the sun, and flocks of birds settled and rose from them. It was a fair day, with clouds scuttling across the sky. The steeple of the church in Boston shimmered faintly, far in the distance. The argument and the three flights had taken their toll, and it took a while for the peace of the setting to still my pounding heart.

I thought about what Simon might have meant, and how I could

21

search for the book. I watched a small puff of dust move toward the castle along the Boston Way.

The road curved along the Witham River in several places, and trees lined it, so it was hard to make out who was coming. The puff grew larger. It had to be horses or a carriage to raise that much dust. It could be one of the castle villagers coming back from the market, but it was moving too quickly. As far as I knew, the Earl and his family were in the castle. There was also another little puff of dust further behind.

As I watched, I could make out fast-moving horses and red jackets. I knew what they were. I ran down the stairs as fast as I could, slipping on the turns of the stone stairs, to the second floor and Father's office.

"Father, the Sheriff's men are coming," I gasped.

# CHAPTER FIVE

FATHER WAS ALWAYS organized, which he related to the military background he was always telling us about.

"Quick, run to the guard house and tell Erik to raise the drawbridge. Then hurry to Simon and tell him to burn any of our papers that could cause trouble. Then go to your mother and tell her to slow them down at the moat. I'll find the Earl."

I ran down the stairs and out the door and across the castle grounds to the moat.

"Raise the drawbridge," I said, my voice hoarse to my own ears. Erik, the fat guardsman, lounging, a smell of ale on his breath, looked at me as though I had lost my senses. The moat had not been closed for months, and I was not a person to give him orders.

"Damnation. By command of the Earl. The Sheriff is coming."

He turned pale, and began to work the ropes that raised the bridge.

I ran back up to find Simon and passed my mother coming down the stairs. Father had already told her about the moat. Simon was no longer in the library, but I found him in his own small office on the second floor. He grasped the problem instantly and began flinging papers every which way. Since it was May, there was no fire in the fireplace. He thrust a pile of papers and a book into my arms and told me to run to Cook's fire. Again, I sped down the stairs, heading toward the kitchen. It was about a hundred feet from the castle in a building made of gray stone instead of brick. The kitchen was outside the castle, of course, to protect against a fire from the ovens spreading and burning everything down.

"Where are you going in such a speed, young Anne?" Cook has always treated me like I was her child, and saved special treats for me.

"No time to talk, just let me throw these things on the fire. The Sheriff is coming."

Her smooth broad face crumpled into worry. "Ah, what will happen now?"

Everyone knew of the tax, and that the Earl had not paid it.

I pushed past Cook and placed Simon's papers and the book on top of the fire. I hated to burn a precious book, but there was no choice. The flames licked the very top of the hearth, the fire so big it was suspicious in itself. I hoped it would die down before the lawmen came. I left the kitchen and went outside to watch.

Patience had come out as well. We could hear the Sheriff's men shouting angrily around the guard house.

"Open, open, in the name of the law!"

Patience grabbed my hand and we stood. "Mother has sent Erik away and is managing the ropes herself," Patience said.

We could hear Mother crying out to the Sheriff's men. "It has caught. I cannot loosen it." She looked helpless.

"She is magnificent," Patience said.

I nodded. I had never admired her more. "Has Father come down from seeing the Earl?"

As I asked, Father emerged from the castle, his arms full. He went into the kitchens and when he came out, without the papers, he called to Erik to go out and lower the drawbridge.

Patience and I hurried back into the kitchen before Father could redirect us. It was a good listening place, through the open door.

We did not have to wait long. The Earl emerged from the castle, looking young and ill at ease, with Father at his side. Father handles most difficult situations for him, but no doubt Father had said it would be best if the Sheriff were greeted by the lord of the manor himself.

The Earl had put on a robe of maroon velvet trimmed in ermine, which made him look like royalty. It also looked hot, since it was now past noon. I had missed the midday meal, and the sun was high in the sky.

The Sheriff and his men galloped over the drawbridge, with that huge hollow noise that hoofs make on a bridge. The Earl and Father walked slowly toward them, as though there were no hurry. The Sheriff's men made a show of stopping suddenly, by drawing the horses around in a circle at the last minute.

The Sheriff, a large man with a belly, got off his horse with a little difficulty. The sun glinted on his fat, red face, and his small eyes had to squint a little. The men were close enough that we could hear them. The Sheriff took off his hat as he approached the Earl and Father. He made a low bow and said, "Greetings, My Lord," to the Earl, and nodded to Father.

My breath came more normally. Perhaps nothing bad would happen. The Earl welcomed the Sheriff and his men to the castle in a polite way, and introduced my father. The Sheriff responded graciously as well. Although the Sheriff was the Law and the representative of the King, the Earl owned a great portion of the shire and made the decisions about the people on it, some of them probably relatives of the Sheriff.

Patience, who was holding my hand tightly in her own, whispered, "Maybe it will be all right." While she was speaking, a carriage with the insignia of the crown rolled up over the moat and came to a stop behind the Sheriff. It must have been the other puff of dust I had seen from the roof.

My heart sank. The carriage meant they were going to take somebody away.

At that moment the Sheriff shut his eyes, opened them, and spoke very fast.

"For non-payment of taxes, I hereby arrest you, Earl of Lincoln, in the name of our sovereign, King Charles I."

At this, Patience squeezed my hand so tightly I cried out in pain. Cook, behind us, began to weep.

"Oh, what of Father, what of Father." I spoke my thoughts out loud. I realized how much I loved him.

"You may get some things together," the Sheriff said.

My father asked how long the Earl would be gone. The Sheriff shrugged and shook his head, "Who knows?" Then, to the Earl, "You may take one man servant. We must search the castle."


THE NEXT HOUR passed in a blur. The Sheriff's men ran through the castle looking at all the books, though of course most of them could not read their own name. They brought all the papers in the castle—some of which belonged to the Earl and some to Father or Simon—to the Sheriff, who looked through them.

In the meantime, Father and Simon helped the Earl put together books and writing materials to occupy his time. The Geneva Bible went first. I saw Raleigh's History go, without regret, and several other books. The Earl's mother, his wife, Arbella, and the servants bustled about putting clothes into trunks for the carriage. Marianne ran up and down stairs with quantities of linen. Cook managed to put in a meat pie that she had baked that afternoon. The whole household, and most of the castle village, thronged inside the castle gates when it was time to leave.

As the livery men put the trunks on the carriage, the Earl's mother, Elizabeth, an old woman in a black dress, drew herself up.

"Where are you taking him?" she demanded of the Sheriff.

We had all assumed he was going to the local court in Boston.

"To the Tower of London, Ma'am," he replied.

The old woman turned pale and reached out for the arm of an attendant.

"Perhaps now others will pay what they owe." As the Sheriff's large, black horse pawed the ground, eager to be off, the Sheriff did not take his eyes off my father.

# Chapter Six

I WENT TO the castle roof to watch the party ride away. The sun was now setting, but I could still see shadows move along the road in the red light from the glow on the horizon. I sat there for a long time after they had passed out of sight, confused, afraid, and sick to my stomach.

I knew about the Tower of London from stories and pictures, though I had never been to London. Father said London was a sea of dirt and pestilence, crowds of people, perhaps two hundred thousand of them, impossible to imagine, all pushing and shoving each other off the walkways into the filth of the street. He said if we minded the smell of the moat, we would faint away at the stench of London. Gentlemen and ladies always had pomanders pressed to their noses. I had seen the Earl's wife give him one. The Earl had been to London, but this time would be different. I tried to imagine, from Father's descriptions, what would happen to him.

The Sheriff's men would take him over London Bridge, with its hundred shops and houses built right onto the bridge and jutting out over the water. Beggars dressed in rags would tap at the carriage. Ladies in fine, bright clothes would saunter with baskets on their arm, buying gloves and silks. Perhaps there would be a bear baiter and a bear. It would be a spectacle, until he looked up and saw the poles on the Great South Gate, with the severed heads of so-called traitors, other Puritans and Catholics also, any who had chosen their faith over the Church of England. Some of the heads would be only skulls, and some would be parboiled and tanned. The Earl's blood would freeze to think that his own head might be among them soon.

Then he would see the Tower, massive, dark-gray stone, not like our own cheerful brick castle. I had seen pictures of the grim Tower with hardly any windows. Many entered and few left, except to the execution block. I thought of how many of the Puritan martyrs had been held in the Tower, and shivered.


I HEARD STEPS on the stairs, and Patience appeared.

"It is time for supper." Patience knows where to find me when I am missing.

"I do not feel like food."

"Mother says we must eat."

"You were right to worry about the Earl," I said as we hurried down. She just shook her head, as if to say it did not matter who was right. She looked woebegone, and I wanted to hug her, to comfort us both, but there was no time.

I slipped into my place on the bench alongside Sarah, to mind her, with Father in his chair at the head and Mother at the foot. Patience and Baby Mercy sat on the bench on the other side. On the table there was only a tureen of soup and a loaf of bread.

Under her breath, Mother said, "Outdoor kitchens, up three huge flights, everything gets spilled, food always cold, so much waste, a castle is to keep the enemy out, not to live in."

"What's that?" Father asked.

"Nothing. The soup was spilled, and it is cold."

Father rose from his chair, his cheeks flushed.

"You care about cold soup at a time like this? What is wrong with you, woman? Always carping and carrying on, even when our lives are crumbling around us."

Father did not usually rage at Mother, at least not in front of us children. Patience turned pale, and Baby Mercy looked like she would cry. Father did not understand that, when Mother was upset, she turned to the things she knew best. Two years ago, after Sarah almost drowned in the moat, Mother went through all the chests in the house and rearranged our clothes.

"May I speak? I felt so much esteem for Mother at the moat today." Ordinarily I would not speak unless spoken to, but it was urgent. Once Father began a rant he could go on forever.

He sank back into his chair. "True, you were as good as a man today at the moat, Dorothy. Better, for they would not have believed that a man could have been so confused about the ropes."

Mother stared at him, and I could not read her face. Was she pleased with the compliment or was she angry at the backhand slap in it? I could not tell.

Father went on for a bit, about what had happened, how lucky we were that he himself had not been taken. "Sometimes it is good fortune to have one's nobility not a thing of common knowledge."

Father was always implying that we had noble blood, but that he could not tell us about it.

"Can they hang him?" Sarah asked. Her voice sounded almost excited.

"Commoners are hung, lords have their heads cut off," Father explained. "It is possible, but they must try him first."

"When will that happen?" Mother asked.

"Who knows? There is a limit to how long a man can be held without trial."

Father began to talk about *habeas corpus*, the principle that you

30

must bring people to trial without imprisoning them indefinitely. His hands were moving rapidly around, and he was drinking large swigs of ale.

I still had no appetite and was playing with my soup. I looked about and saw Patience sadly looking off into space. Baby Mercy was making balls out of the white portions of her bread. Sarah kicked me under the table, for no particular reason I could see other than ill humor.

A change of topic would help. "Father, I thought today, when Mother was at the moat, about what you have told us about the moat at Amiens."

Father responded. "I know I have told you of the Spanish general, short and withered and yellow, with a red beard."

We all nodded.

"And how he took Amiens in half an hour?"

He went on with his story about how the Spanish general had invaded the walled city of Amiens, accessible only through a drawbridge over the moat. First the general hid fifteen thousand Spanish soldiers in a nearby wood. Then he dressed a dozen French-speaking Spaniards as peasants, and gave them bags of walnuts to sell near the drawbridge. The French guards were being especially careful about letting down the drawbridge, and conducted a thorough search of each vehicle.

After the guards had finished questioning the driver of one wagon, they lowered the drawbridge to let him enter. At that moment the walnut sellers spilled several sacks of nuts underfoot. Everyone scrambled to pick them up, and the cart and the guards began to slip on the nuts. In the confusion the walnut sellers took control of the ropes on the gate. One of them let out a shrill whistle, and the Spanish soldiers came out of hiding and sped through the gate into town. Since it was Sunday, the French were at church, and there was no resistance. There were hardly any dead.

I had heard the story several times before, but perhaps because of the Sheriff's men in their uniforms demanding entrance over our own moat, this time it felt more real. I could see the walnuts scampering over the cobbled road and the guards slipping on them. I could hear the whistle and see the red banners snapping in the wind as the horse-soldiers galloped in. I imagined a smell of fear in the town, not so different from the smell around our table.

We girls were excused. As I went to my room I heard Mother's voice raised.

"Old stories do not help us now. You must pay the tax. There is no question."

Father's voice roared back, "Have you no conscience, woman? No feeling? The young Earl, whom I advised not to pay the tax, has been dragged to the Tower, and you believe that I should betray him and my principles so that I am saved."

"I am thinking only of the children."

"You are thinking of yourself."

I could hear Father walking around and I hurried away so that he would not find me listening. I thought that he would not pay the tax, whatever Mother said.

THAT NIGHT AS we went to sleep, Patience and I hugged each other for a moment. We were both quiet. I did not know if I could sleep, but I must have been very tired. I felt myself falling, soon, with thoughts of all the events of the day swirling through my mind, including my talk with Simon.

I woke up with a start and said, "Patience, there is a secret room in the castle!"

"Um." She was asleep, and I had to shake her a little to get her to listen.

I told her about my conversation with Simon.

"What could he have meant about rabbits?"

"I don't know. The only rabbit in the castle that I know is the one on the mantle of the fireplace, on the second floor."

At that, I sat up. "Patience, that must be it. I must go and see."

Each floor of the castle had a huge stone fireplace, and they all had carvings on the mantel. The man who built Tattershall Castle was the King's treasurer, and so many of the decorations around the castle were purses—not interesting. But the carvings on the second-floor fireplace were of animals and flowers, and among them there was a rabbit.

Patience begged me to stay in bed, reminding me how angry Father would be if I were found looking for secret rooms at a time when the whole castle was supposed to be grieving for the Earl. She did not say anything about being selfish, but I knew from her tone that was what she meant.

I was too excited to stay in bed. This would be a good time, when few people might be around.

I had worn my shift to bed, as always, and did not trouble to put anything over it. I picked up the candle I had left on our chest when we went to bed, although there was no fire to light it from. I opened the door slowly.

THE HALL WAS completely black. Bits of light filtered into the outside rooms from the stars and moon, but in the halls there was no light at all. I felt my way along, the bricks clammy against my hand. I stumbled once or twice, but the way was straight, and I found the staircase. The stone was cold on my bare feet. Stone stairs at least do not creak like wooden ones, so I made no sound. Not until I stumbled and missed the last two steps, landing with a jolt and a pain in my heel. I stifled the curse that came to my lips. Mother was right to complain about the uneven steps.

When I reached the second floor, there was a dim light, and I saw that someone had left a candle guttering on the mantel. Now I could see my way. There seemed to be nobody about, and I walked as quietly as I could to the fireplace.

I had noticed before that the rabbit was slightly more polished than the other carvings, as though people had reached out to touch it for many years; I had thought for luck, but perhaps it was something else.

I touched the ears and nothing happened. I tried to wiggle them backwards and forwards, in every possible direction, but they did not move. Then I tried pulling them as though I were going to lift the rabbit off the mantel. I felt them move, just a little, and I heard a slight sound to my left. My heart leapt. I could not see anything.

The walls of the room, like most of the castle, were covered with tapestries to brighten the walls and make them warmer in winter. Perhaps there was something under the tapestry?

I was frightened of what I might find, and frightened that somebody might come, but I lit my candle from the one on the mantel, lifted the tapestry on the left, closest to the fireplace, and moved under it.

It was hard to breathe, under the dusty hanging, as I crept along. And then I found a door. There was a door! Just a shabby little door, and it was ever so slightly ajar, as though a latch had been released when I pulled the rabbit ears. I gave it a little push, and it moved an inch or so, creaking loudly. I took a deep breath and pushed it hard.

It was a small room with a small window. I could faintly smell the necessary in the corner. I held the candle up and I could see that the walls were covered with faded red hangings, so dilapidated that shreds of them were falling on the floor. There was a bed in the corner, with wool blankets on it, and a stool. Under the window a large oak chest stood, much like the one in our room, but covered with strange carvings. Men and beasts were fighting, and the roots of trees trapped all of them. It was the only place in the room where books could be hidden, yet I felt uncomfortable approaching it.

I told myself not to be fanciful, put the candle on the floor, and knelt before the chest. The lid was heavy. I struggled, using my weight to push it up. The lid hit the stone wall with a bang, and I saw revealed perhaps twenty books.

Here was the treasure! I began to pull them out, holding them close to the candle so I could read the titles. *The Decameron*, *The Poems of Sappho*, Chaucer's *Canterbury Tales*, Horace's *Odes*, a slim book called *Tis Pity She's a Whore*, and a few other thin books that I knew could not be what I wanted.

There were only a few left, on the bottom. I took the largest, bound in brown leather. *The First Folio: Works of Wm Shakespeare*, flickered in gold on the front.

I put the book on the bed and lay next to it, holding the candle in one hand. It was too awkward, so I closed the trunk, placed Shakespeare on it, and put the candle on the trunk as well. By pulling the stool up to the trunk, I could read. I had no thought of bringing the book away. I could barely carry it and there was no place I could hide it.

There were many plays. I found *Romeo and Juliet* and discovered the place where I had left off, at the fair. Soon I was totally absorbed. When I got to the ending tears streamed down my face. I was happy.

Then I went back to the beginning, which I had missed as well, and read about Romeo, and how he had loved another before he met Juliet. It was cool in the room, and I hugged my knees under my long shift to keep warm. Just as I got to the place where they were meeting at the dance, I glanced up and realized it was getting light outside. I wanted so much to know what would happen at the dance. It reminded me of the young man at the fair.

Reluctantly, I closed the book. I replaced all the books in the chest, pulled the door shut, and made my way back, the fabric of the tapestry scratching against my face. The return in the partial light was easier than my dark journey down. When I got to the room, Patience was asleep, and I tried not to disturb her, but the instant I sat on our straw mattress to swing my legs up she was wide awake. I told her everything, about the secret room and the play, and by the time I had finished there was scarcely any point in going to sleep.

# Chapter Seven

When we got up it was time for morning prayers. Because the whole town was grieving for the Earl, we went across the way to the village church, instead of our usual services in the castle chapel.

We made a procession with the Earl's sister, Lady Arbella, and her husband leading the way; then Lady Elizabeth, the Earl's mother, escorted by one of her other sons who had arrived in the night after hearing the news; then the Earl's wife and children; and then Father and Mother and Simon. Finally, Sarah and Patience and Baby Mercy and I came, and behind us the personal servants to the Earl and his family.

We walked along the moat. The smell was terrible, in spite of the two channels cut into it to carry the waste water away. The channels were very narrow, only about a foot and a half wide, too narrow to allow intruders access to the castle by boat. My brother Sam, however, had used the channels a year or two ago, to escape from the castle when he wanted to go out at night and knew our parents would not let him. He would wait until dark, drop from his room on a rope tied to the window, and go to his tiny punt, hidden under the weeds near the outdoor kitchen.

Sam and a friend from the village used to take the boat through the fens. He had told me that he could get to the River Bain, and then to the Witham, which runs all the way to Boston, though it required a lot of poling through weeds. There was a tavern on the river that he and Charles favored over the one at the castle village. If they became rowdy, Father would have less chance of hearing about it. I thought of all this when I saw the corner of the punt peeking out from the weeds. I wondered whether Sam had heard the news about the Earl, at college, and if he would come home.

We walked through the castle yard, over the moat on the drawbridge, and into the outer yards of the castle village—then past the stables, the carriage house, the housing for the guards, and some abandoned buildings from earlier times.

Then we were in the village proper, where the tenant farmers had their huts. We went by the tavern, the blacksmith, the ironmonger, and Davey's bakery where I sometimes went for a roll. The smell of baking bread and the scent of some early wild roses helped to mask the smell of the moat.

As I entered the church with Sarah's hand in mine, I looked up and saw a spot of rat-brown color from the corner of my eye. I turned to see, standing at some distance, the beggar man from the fair. He was with the villagers hanging about the tavern. I had not thought of him in days, but there he was. I stopped dead in my tracks, Sarah stumbled and pulled my arm, and I almost fell. When I looked again the beggar was gone. Sarah called me a niggle-headed puppy, but my mind was in another place.

The service was mournful. We sang two sad hymns, and the Reverend spoke about how, in the end, God sets everything right. I wondered. If God is so just and powerful, how did it happen that the Earl would be taken from his family, leaving us in grief? I offered up a prayer from my heart for the Earl, his family, and us all. I watched a bat as it swirled through the dark part of the belfry. When the minister was finished, the Earl's family left first, then my father, then Simon, and then I pushed in front of the others, leaving

38

Sarah to fend for herself. I looked around for the beggar man and could not find him. I thought I saw a flash of brown round the tavern, but that was all.

Rufus, a small boy with bright-red hair, a son of one of the tenants, came forward and said something to my father that I could not hear. Father's voice was gruff. He turned to Simon, who followed Rufus behind the tavern.

I tried to follow, but Mother spoke sharply to me, and I had to come back. We returned to the castle and climbed the stairs to breakfast. After some time Simon appeared, went to Father at the head of the table, leaned over, and spoke into his ear. I could hear only one word, "man," which told me nothing. Father pushed his plate away and rose abruptly. Without saying a word, the two of them left the rest of us sitting there.

Mother had to tell me to finish the bread and cheese on my plate.


WHEN WE WERE excused, I immediately went down to the library for my lessons. Simon was nowhere to be found. Since Raleigh's *History* was gone, I found a book of verse and sat there turning the pages, seeing nothing. Finally Simon appeared, looking distracted.

"What is happening?" I asked.

"What do you mean?" Simon said.

"Something is going on."

No matter what I said, Simon would tell me nothing. Finally he said, "Stop asking."

I hated when Simon acted as a father. It was all right when I was a child, but now I felt I should be treated like an equal.

I wanted to leave the room, slamming the door, but I did not dare. I sat and stared angrily at my book. Why wouldn't he tell me?

Later in the afternoon I helped Mother stuff a pillow with goose feathers. It was a rare, sunny day without a cloud, and we sat outside.

It was hot, and I had bits of feather sticking to all of my clothes and hair. I felt as if I were stewing like a capon. Then I remembered that I had just found a secret room and read a secret play. I did not need my family to include me, in order to find excitement. I could go back to the room that very night and read the beginning of *Romeo and Juliet*, which I had missed.

I was tired from the night before, but I was also tired of worrying about my health. I would just do it. I finished stitching up the pillow and, as Simon walked by, I threw it at him. He jumped, then tossed it back to me. Mother told me to be more ladylike.

That night when Patience and I went to bed, I did not tell her of my plans. I stayed awake for a bit and felt myself dozing off. Wake up at two! Wake up at two! I said to myself.

I WOKE WHEN the church clock struck two. I was pleased with myself, although I don't know how I did it.

I got out of bed silently, took our unlit candle, and retraced the journey I had made the night before, which seemed easier this night. As I walked down the dark halls, I thought I heard someone behind me. I hid behind the closest tapestry, stifling a cough from the dust. It sounded like footsteps in the large room and then the noise stopped. After a bit I told myself I had imagined it, or that it was only mice.

I emerged from the tapestry and walked slowly in the dark along the wall to the stairs. Then I went down to the fireplace, found a candle burning again, and lit my own. Once there was light, I saw the rabbit ears.

I pulled the tapestry back from the walls and stepped under. When I reached the door I paused for a moment, feeling proud, then pushed the door open with a dramatic shove. It banged on the wall behind.

There was a loud noise, a sort of curse, something on the bed moved, and I was thrust against the wall with a large hand choking my neck and a knife raised over my head. Angry eyes, dark blue, stared into mine for an instant till I dropped the candle.

I heard a laugh. My neck was released, and I sank to the floor, sitting with my back against the wall. My knees were too weak to stand.

"Only a girl."

"Who are you?" I asked.

"I would rather know who you are."

He had somehow caught my candle, which thankfully had not gone out. He held it above my head as he studied me.

"I am Anne Dudley, daughter of Thomas Dudley."

I tried to sound dignified, but it was hard to be dignified sitting on the floor in my shift, my voice breaking from the tension.

He was also in his shift. I had never been so close to a man, before, with so few clothes between us. The smell of his body, when he had shoved me against the wall, was like garden herbs in the sun, and made me feel dizzy.

He was a young man, in his early twenties. He had obviously been asleep, and his long dark hair was all askew. He had not shaved in several days. I had never seen a man so handsome.

"Well, sit down on my stool."

The hand that pulled me from the floor was strong and hard. I settled myself on the stool, pulling my shift down over my legs as far as it would go. I felt his eye upon me and knew I was blushing. He put the candle on the floor and sat on his bed among the rumpled blankets. His shift was short, and I could see a great deal of his muscular legs with their dark hair.

"You have not told me who you are."

He did not reply for a moment.

"It could be dangerous to know me," he said then.

"I already know you."

I was not quite sure what I meant but for the feeling of his hand, as he had pulled me up, and the sweet smell of his body.

He smiled, and even in the dim light his face changed entirely, from fierce, hard lines to something softer.

"I am John Holland."

"Oh." I knew the name. "You are the Earl's Steward for his home at Sempringham."

We had stayed at Sempringham some years ago, before Father had moved the family to Boston. It was one of the Earl's properties, the ruins of an old monastery, with two lovely houses built around it. Mother much preferred Sempringham to the castle. When Father was not available, the Earl hired John Holland as his Steward.

"What are you doing here in this secret room? Are you the secret my father and Simon have been whispering about?"

He nodded. "Probably. I'm hiding from the Sheriff."

He explained that it was he who had written the tract, circulated everywhere, about how no one should pay an unlawful tax. It was the paper posted in the market last Sunday. When the King had sent out the warrant for the Earl, he had also made out a warrant for John.

"So you think no one should pay the tax?"

He got up from the bed and began to pace up and down in the little room, swinging his arms. If the King had been there he should have had a bloody nose, I was sure.

"That puny, lily-livered, paper-faced, boil-brained piece of suet, to go against the people of this country, disbanding the Parliament, declaring a war for his own pride, a Catholic in Church of England clothes. No right-thinking Englishman will pay this tax!"

I could see why the King wanted to lock him up.

"And do you know a beggar in a rat-brown cloak?" I thought I should change the subject.

"What do you know of him, young woman?" He was standing over me.

42

My knees were still weak, and my heart still beating faster than it should.

"I know little." My voice quavered again, and I stopped and spoke more firmly. "I saw him at the fair, and I saw him today, and I wondered why he was so far from Boston. He frightens me."

"Hmph. That one goes everywhere."

"What shall you do?"

"Go to Holland."

"Like the pilgrims," I said.

He nodded. "And maybe someday I shall go to the New World. Like them."

"There is nothing there, no towns, no houses, nothing, only endless wilderness, and heathen Indians and wild animals waiting to kill you." I could not imagine a worse fate.

He smiled and his face relaxed again. "I prefer to think of it as an adventure."

He was not so much older than I, surely younger than Simon. My heart stirred, perhaps at the idea of the adventure, or perhaps only at his blue eyes.

"How long shall you be here?" I hoped it would be long.

"Till a boat arrives in Boston that is going to Holland and will take me."

"That could be tomorrow or next month," I said.

"Should you like me to stay longer?"

This time, he not only smiled, he smiled at me. I felt myself blush again. I stood up from the stool and said I must go back to my room.

"What shall I tell your father about your visit?"

I began to beg him, speaking of my father's temper, until I saw he was teasing me.

"What brought you here?"

I wondered what he would think of me, a girl who wanted to read lewd books, but I told him about *Romeo and Juliet*, and he laughed.

"Have you found the books, also?" I asked.

He nodded and pointed to *The Canterbury Tales* lying beside the bed.

"I will think of something to say to your father so that we shall meet again," he said as I left.

I made my way back up the stairs to my room, so many different feelings running through me. I fell down beside Patience, wanting to wake her so I could talk to her, and wanting her to stay asleep so that I could hug my excitement to myself.

# Chapter Eight

I was tempted to tell Patience in the morning, but I did not. I had never felt so drawn to a man before. I had not even seen many men, outside of tenant farmers and fishermen who, for the most part, never bathed, and had no learning, and nothing to talk about except turnips and eels.

John had been reading Chaucer, and his body was clean. That was only the beginning of who he was.

I was impatient to see him again and waited all day for something to happen. I walked to the Church and tried to still my unholy thoughts. The rest of the day I spent in the library, looking off into space. I kept reliving moments, especially what John had said about a scheme so we could meet again. Perhaps he had not meant it, or perhaps he had failed.

I went to bed sadly, knowing that I could sneak off to the secret room again on my own, and wondering what John would think; probably that I was too forward. As I was taking off my outer clothes, Patience already in the bed, there was a knock on our door. I peered around it so only my head could be seen. It was Seymour, a tall, thin servant, who told me to go to my father's office at once. I threw my skirts back over my shift and ran down the stairs, my hands damp from the exertion and from excitement.

FATHER SAT BEHIND his table and looked stern. "Hmm. There is something I wish to tell you. Something I wish you to do, in fact. But it is also a matter of which you cannot speak to anyone, not to Patience or Sarah or even your mother."

He was looking down at the table and he kept rubbing his nose.

"Mother does not know?"

"Mother knows."

The silence that followed told me that Mother did not approve.

"Does Simon know?"

"Simon knows. He is the only other one, and it must stay that way."

I swore secrecy, but Father still said nothing of what was happening, although he continued to talk about the need for secrecy, with a great many "Hmm's" and rubbings of his nose.

"What is the secret, Father?" I finally asked outright.

"We have a guest." Silence.

"A guest," I prompted.

And then finally he told me about John, although not so much as John himself had said the night before. He did say that John was wanted by the King for treason, and that it was extremely important to keep his presence a secret because we could all be arrested for treason for keeping him. "He is a hothead, but we both oppose the King's tax."

I asked what he meant, and he said only that our guest could be impulsive. At the end, he said he was telling me because someone needed to bring food to the guest.

"Tonight I carried him a tray, and all the servants I met on the stair looked at me strangely. You could carry food without anyone thinking it odd."

At that moment I was glad to be a girl.

"I made up a story to tell Cook, which I am certain she did not believe. Also John, that is his name, thought my choice of food somewhat odd."

"What did you bring, Father?"

"A joint of meat and a raisin tart."

"Nothing to drink and no bread nor vegetables?"

Father reddened a little. "What does it matter? From now on, you can do it. Start tomorrow night. Just once a day, that will be enough; people should not see you come and go. You must wait till midnight tomorrow to carry the tray in. Get the tray from Cook, saying it is for Patience, who is ill. And tell Patience she must stay out of Cook's way."

"What can I tell Patience? She will want to know why."

"Whatever you like, but not the truth."

I was speechless. Father always said we must speak the truth above all else, and now he was telling me to lie.

He seemed to read my face and he waved his hand impatiently. "Take a lesson from Sarah."

I blushed, for it was just what I was thinking.

"Of course, I want you to bring the tray in and curtsey and leave. You are not to talk to him."

I blushed again as I said, "Yes, Father."

"And speaking of Sarah, make sure she does not see you. She is so thoughtless and wayward, she would have the Sheriff's men upon us in no time."

The mention of the Sheriff sobered me. This was not just a game so I could be with a young man.

"If we were found out, we might have to flee to the fens, ourselves. These marshes around us have held so many outlaws, from Robin Hood till today. The fens are almost impassable, but I know you do not want to live among wet, cold reeds."

I was stunned at the idea that our family could live in the marshes, but as Father went on about Robin Hood and other outlaws, past and present, my mind began to wander. He brought himself up short and began to tell me about the secret room, and how to enter it, in great detail. It gave me practice in lying, to keep my face straight and ask innocent questions.

"There is a rabbit head on the fireplace?"

When I left Father's office I felt like skipping, something I have not done since childhood. How delightful life seemed, and how exciting! I had forgotten again about the Sheriff's men.

I had a hard time falling asleep. I kept thinking of John, behind the tapestry, gnawing on the joint Father had brought him. I wondered if he had spoken to Father, or if it had been Father's idea that I should bring the food. I had not dared to ask.

My happy impatience continued through the next day. It was raining, a hard rain that we seldom see. Usually it mists and sprinkles and clears for a bit and then mists again. This day, the rain came down like God was pouring out the washing water from a huge pail in the sky. There was no going up to the roof of the castle to distract myself.

I went to the library. Simon was sitting in his chair at the large oak table, and I sat down at my own small table. I asked Simon if he would find me another book, poetry if possible. To my surprise, he came directly to my table and pulled a leaflet out of his jacket, saying he had received it in Boston last Sunday. The leaflet was by a young man named Milton, who Simon said was a good Puritan not much older than I. It made me think I could someday write poems myself. We spent some time looking at the rhyme and meter and talking of the ideas in the poems, mainly religious, but there was one about love.

"Interesting that this young Puritan should find his mind turning to thoughts of love," I said.

Simon turned away, and I could see his neck growing red.

"Perhaps when you have written this many fine pieces about God's love, you also will have time to think of human love. In the meantime, diagram the meter in this one."

He picked the most difficult poem, put it in front of me, and went back to his place. Before I knew, my head had fallen to the table. For several days I had not slept well, what with midnight excursions and too much thinking.

When I woke, Simon was standing over me. "I let you sleep for half an hour."

He brushed my apologies aside. "I used the time to write something for you."

He handed me a sheet of paper. He had written something on the back of one of John's flyers about not paying the King's tax. I took it, and began to read.

> *Anne Dudley has asked a "wicked" question. She wants to know how to treat Catholics, as our Puritan faith tells us we should not tolerate them. It is wickedly hard to answer this question."*

"Let us discuss it another time," Simon said. "Just read it through quickly now."

I skimmed the phrases.

> *Basis of religion is embracing God's mercy as a principle of living... Importance of teaching those with other beliefs but not forcing them against their will... Religion must be freely chosen... Truth will show itself... We seek religious freedom, we should therefore offer it to others... Our King, the idiot dwarf, must learn these principles, or else England's future shall be a civil war of bloodshed unending...*

Simon seated himself on the bench beside me. His eyes glowed and he looked younger than usual. I felt an urge to reach out to touch his arm. I remembered John in the secret room and felt strangely guilty, not sure if the feeling was because of Simon or because of John.

He began to talk about the pilgrims, who escaped from England and went first to Leiden, in Holland, and then to the New World. As I knew, they were different from us Puritans. Pilgrims felt that other religions should be tolerated, while Reverend Cotton and most other Puritans felt that we have the one Truth and should not accept others among us who might cause us to waver in our beliefs.

"If we have the one Truth," I said, "then it should hold against any other argument. We should not be threatened by what others say or believe."

His face shone. "Nothing you could have said could give me more pleasure." He began to study my face. "There is something changed in you in the last days."

"I am very tired," I said. I could not tell him about John.

At that moment the door opened and Mother entered, telling me to come help her with the meal.

I slipped John's paper into the back of the Milton leaflet and said loudly, "I find the poem about God's goodness especially moving."

Simon grunted some reply and went back to his chair.

I told Mother I must run to my room first, and I took the Milton pages with me, intending to read Simon's paper more carefully in private and to return it to him. Generally we left the books in the library, as they were too valuable to leave around the castle where a servant might be tempted to pick them up. I left the book in my room, under the bed, and went back to help.

When I reached our dining room I saw Father was not with us. I thought he was probably eating with the Earl's family. He had said that Arbella was in need of counsel without her brother's presence.

50

I looked at the large tureens of food upon the sideboard, and I thought of a better plan than my father's.

I said, bold as you please, "Father asked me to make up a plate for him."

I gave Mother a significant look. She said nothing. Father had said to ask Cook for food, for Patience, but I had worried that Cook might only give me a small bowl of gruel, since Patience was supposed to be sick. John needed a good deal of food and drink. I piled a trencher high with roasted duck, bread, a stew of spring greens with thyme, and a piece of early cherry pie, adding a tankard of ale.

At the end of the meal, I took it to my room. I would have to think of something to tell Patience about the food. My mind went back and forth about what to say, until we went to bed.

I put the plate under the bed, beside the Milton book, and hoped for the best.

As Patience walked around the bed ready to get into it, her candle in hand and ready to blow it out, she sniffed and said, "What is that smell? It smells like duck."

It had occurred to me that she would smell the food, but what could I say? The best I managed was, "You have strange fancies."

"No, I declare I smell a roasted duck."

Before I could say anything further, she was wandering around the room, searching for food. It did not take her long to find the trencher under the bed.

"What is this? This is the plate you took for Father from dinner."

"Father changed his mind."

"So why didn't you take it back to the kitchen? It will draw mice."

"You know I am trying to gain weight. I thought I might be hungry in the night."

"When have you ever been hungry in the night? You cannot keep food under my bed. I do not want mice running over me."

I was beginning to run out of ideas. Lying was hard. "In fact, I did not want to tell you, but it is something Simon told me about. It is a strange Catholic ritual, like Communion. I will get up in the middle of the night and eat the food and then make a wish."

"That is the silliest thing I have ever heard. You are lying."

So I told her the truth as we lay in the bed. The rain had stopped, the sky was clear, and a part of the moon was visible through our window. The night was so warm I threw off my coverlet. Patience made sounds of wonder and scolded me for not having told her before. It was good to have someone to talk to about what John looked like and what I had felt.

"But you cannot marry an outlaw."

Patience is always practical. I had not got so far in my thinking to reach marriage.

"No, and even if I could, he is probably going off to America, and I should never want to do that."

Patience shuddered. "To give up our castle, our bed so warm we need no covers, to live with bears and wolves and lions."

Nothing she said could have been better preparation for taking the food to John. I had no intention of curtseying and leaving without a word, but I vowed to keep my distance from a man whom I could never marry.

# CHAPTER NINE

I FELL SOUNDLY asleep, and would have slept through the twelve o'clock church bell, but Patience heard it and woke me. I put on a rose-colored skirt I liked, over my shift. It was not my best one, which would look like I was primping.

I heard a rustle as I leaned under the bed to gather my tray. Patience was right, the mice had found the trencher. I could not see how much damage they had done in the night, without a candle, but I picked up the plate and made my way downstairs. This night, I heard nothing in the halls or staircase and I went easily to the secret room.

John had a candle already lit and he was sitting on his bed, dressed this time. He was wearing blue—dark blue trousers over a light blue shift. It made me notice the blue of his eyes all over again. Blue eyes with dark hair are so rare, and especially handsome. I wondered if he had thought of me, as he dressed, the way that I had thought of him when I chose the rose skirt. Most likely he was already dressed, and the blue clothes were all that he had.

I placed the tray upon the oak chest. I did not curtsey but I was prepared to say a few words and leave.

"I told you I should find a way to see you again," he said. He explained that he had told my father that he lacked a woman's way with food. Father had taken it to heart, as John had intended.

His smile was just as I had remembered, only sweeter. My resolve weakened.

"And you have brought me a much finer dinner than your father did."

I could see the tray clearly now in the candlelight, and while there were a few suspicious crumbs around the tart, there were no other signs that mice had been there. I decided not to mention mice to John.

He beckoned to the stool, and I found myself sitting on it. Near me on the floor there was a plate with a well-gnawed bone on it.

John was drinking the ale down with a will.

"A day without anything to drink is hard," I said.

"Indeed. And it is hard to be confined to such a small room with nothing to do but read forbidden books."

"Have you read anything interesting?"

He told me about Chaucer and the story of the pilgrims. It sounded quite a proper story to me, and I wondered aloud why the book was in this room.

"Hmm." For a moment John sounded like Father. "Some of the pilgrims, like the wife of Bath, have had adventures that Reverend Cotton would not approve of."

He would not tell me more.

I asked if he had read any Shakespeare.

"No, perhaps tomorrow."

I began to tell him the plot of *Romeo and Juliet*. I stopped with a start. I realized first that I might spoil the story for him, and then that I should not be speaking this way with a man I could not marry. I rose and prepared to leave, taking the platter with the gnawed bone. I left the plate I had brought, as he had not finished it.

"Stay."

It sounded heartfelt, and I wanted to stay, but I forced myself out of the room. I wondered if he was just lonely, or if it was my company in particular that he wanted.

"Tomorrow I will bring more ale," I promised. I had not thought about how much a person drinks in a day.

As I was shutting the door, I met his eyes and could hardly leave. He said softly as he smiled, "Just bring yourself."


THE MOMENT I opened the door to our room, Patience said, "Well?"

"I left after a few moments, just as you said I should."

"But you did talk, I can tell. There is something in your voice."

As we lay there in the dark I told her everything, how John had spoken to Father, and each thing he had said to me, and I to him, and about his smile.

"Anne, you must not fall in love with him, you must not. He will leave and your heart will break."

I said I would certainly not fall in love with him. I knew, even as I said it, that I could not promise any such thing. Patience knew it too, I thought, from the way she squeezed my hand in the dark.

I dreamed that night of a white horse that was wild and running through the marshes. He saw me, stopped, and then approached. I held out an apple in my hand, and he came to me without any fear. I got onto his back, and we raced through the fens so fast I could not see the ground beneath me.

When I woke up the next morning, I remembered that one cannot race through the fens on a horse, as it is too wet, and the horse must go extremely slowly, to avoid getting up to its hocks and breaking them with the sudden movements.

"Dreams are dreams," I said to myself, and got up.

After breakfast mother set Patience and me the task of re-hemming Sarah and Baby Mercy's skirts, since they had grown out of them. It was laborious, as their skirts were so full and there were so many stitches.

Since the day was fine, we sat outside, to the side of the castle on a small knoll where the grass was thick. A breeze carried the flies away, and we sat upwind of the smell from the moat. Sarah and Baby Mercy stayed with us, and Sarah made merry at our expense.

The day before, Mother had put Sarah to lengthening her own skirts. She had made such a mess of the stitches, and the hem had been so uneven on the first skirt, that Mother had taken it from her. She said that however slovenly Sarah was willing to look, she, her mother, did not want to be seen with such a slothful hog of a daughter. Once again, I thought as I pushed the needle through the heavy linen petticoat, pricking my finger; Sarah had gotten her own way.

Strangely, when Sarah wins, she is seldom contrite. Instead, it seems to spur her on to new feats of disobedience and willfulness. She was merciless that day, running up to pull my hair when I was not watching, untying Patience's sash on her skirt over and over like a kitten, and pushing Baby Mercy into the mud at the bottom of the knoll so that she cried and had to have her clothes changed. What was most irksome was that because she and Baby Mercy were there, Patience and I could not talk about what was on our minds, or at least on my mind.

As we sat there in the sun, Patience had to re-thread and she dropped her needle. Cursing herself as a stupid hedgepig, she felt around in the grass and then stood up to go back into the castle for another. Sarah and Mercy decided to go in with her, leaving me a moment's peace.

After Patience had gone, I saw Marianne running away from the basement entrance to the castle, flushed and out of breath. When

I beckoned to her, she stopped running and walked toward me. I asked her what had happened, and she held back a sob.

"Sit for a minute, then."

She flung herself on the grass beside me and told her story. She had encountered Erik, the guardhouse keeper, in the basement where she had been sent to get a pomander for Arbella. Erik had cornered Marianne and tried to kiss her, and only by a quick movement had she managed to slip by him and get away. Once up the basement stairs, she had simply run.

"Just because I am a servant-girl does not mean my morals are loose. This happens so often."

I was angry and said she must tell Arbella. She said she had, but there was little Arbella could do for her except tell her to threaten the men. And now that the Earl was gone, she had even less authority.

"Part of the problem is that you are beautiful."

She waved her hand impatiently. "Beauty is not helping me find a husband. There are only local clods from the village with whom I would always be hungry." She paused, then continued shyly, looking down at the grass as she ran her fingers through it. "Sometimes I dream," she said. She told me about the Earl's visitors and how she had met a lord's valet she fancied.

I told her that to me her dreams sounded as if they could come true.

"But what happens when a man finds out I am Catholic?"

I had no answer. We sat there in silence, her fair face mournful. And then I thought of something.

"Simon! He would not care if you are Catholic. He has just shown me a paper he has written about tolerance."

Her face lit up and she sat up suddenly, her knees bent and showing more of her ankles under the long skirt than was proper. "He would be lovely. He is handsome, and kind, and rich and... don't you fancy him yourself?"

I smiled a little sadly. "I am not blind. I have also noticed that he is handsome, and he has always been kind to me. I have tried many times to capture his fancy, but he never responds. I guess he is too old for me. His ideas are old. He is always talking about politics and history, and often it is boring. He is the teacher, and I am the student."

I told her what happened if I mentioned romance or love to Simon, like about King Charles and his romantic journey, and how he accused me of being a silly, sentimental girl. She laughed.

"You are wrong on one count," I said. "He is not rich."

"In my world he is rich."

I thought she was saying that I did not understand her position, and she was probably right.

"He is above my station, but if you introduced me in the right way it might be possible."

Patience was returning, and Marianne stood up.

"Yes, Simon values intelligence, and I can tell him you are not only beautiful but also intelligent."

She smiled and walked away.

Patience and I sewed and talked and enjoyed the blue sky and puffy clouds and tried to keep Sarah from tormenting Mercy. It was time for the evening meal before I knew.

There was a lovely soup of early summer squash flavored with dill seed, and a mash of peas, and a joint of venison, which we all attacked with a will.

Father, once again, was missing from the table. At the end of the meal, two servants came to carry the food away, so like the night before I took a large empty platter and began to pile it high.

"Who is that for?" asked Sarah. She spoke loud enough that all looked up from the table at me.

"Speak when you are spoken to," I said absently, as I continued to pile mashed peas on the plate. "It is for Father."

"Is not."

I looked up from the peas to see that Sarah was no longer sitting at her place next to mine at the table, but standing up and pointing at me.

"She is lying, Mother. I know she is. She is supposed to be so good, she and Patience, but she is lying. Last night she said the food was for Father and she carried it to her room, and in the morning it was gone!"

I opened my mouth to speak, but no words came out. I looked at Patience, and she too was speechless. Finally Mother came to my rescue.

"Sarah, you graceless child, hold your tongue. What your sister does is no concern of yours. Mind your own Godless behavior— telling tales, speaking to hurt another—or you shall be in deeper trouble than you already are."

I took a deep breath and finished filling the plate as fast as I could. I poured ale into the largest tankard at the table and placed a bowl of soup on the trencher. Balancing the trencher in one hand and holding the tankard in the other, I sped out of the room before Sarah could say anything more.

I took the food and again hid it under my bed. I paced up and down the little room, from the bed to the oak chest to the window to the bed. Two servants had been present when Sarah shouted her accusations. They would talk. Then there were the footsteps I had heard the night before last, when I had gone to the secret room. What if someone had been watching?

It could have been Sarah, but it could also have been servants. If it were known that John was in the house, the Sheriff's men would come to look for him. They would find the secret room if they looked under the tapestries.

I did not love him, no I did not, so why was my heart beating so fast? I wanted to see him, that was all. Midnight would come, but it seemed it would take forever.

# Chapter Ten

Finally midnight came. Once again, I thought I heard someone move as I started down the stairs, but I waited for a minute and then there was quiet. I had a hard time balancing the wooden trencher in the dark—the night before I had not brought soup. I tripped on the uneven stone stairs that Mother was always complaining about, and the platter slipped from my grip. I managed to catch it before it landed on the stairs, but soup spilled all over everything, including me. My green skirt and my arms were wet. I had rubbed rose petals against my forehead and my neck and wrists. Now I would smell of summer squash, not roses.

I opened the door to the secret room to see John standing. He had heard me coming. The room carried his own scent, not of flowers or soup, but just his body.

"Hello."

My voice sounded strange in my ears. The night before, I had been more distant. Tonight I was too full of worry to put on my mask of unconcern.

He was wearing a different shift under his trousers, so he must have brought a change of clothes to the castle. He was not as tall as I had remembered him from the night I had woken him and he had attacked me. I do not know how he had shaved without water, but he had, with one or two cuts on his chin. He took the tray from me and placed it on the chest.

"Sorry, I have spilled the soup."

In the candlelight I could see that the trencher, my arm, and my dress were all covered with light green soup.

"No worry. What a good woman to try to bring me soup!"

I felt myself blush with pleasure, especially at being called a woman.

He sat down on the bed and began again with the ale. I took my place on the stool.

"I was going to bring two tankards but I was in haste."

In a flood of words, I explained what had happened with Sarah and the servants.

He smiled that smile that melted something in me.

"You are worried for me, I can tell."

I blushed again, this time with embarrassment.

"It will be all right. There is always danger of being discovered, even in a secret room. I shall have to leave soon, regardless." He paused. "I will be sorry to leave you."

"I will be sorry, too." My voice broke on the "sorry."

"Come sit beside me. We have such little time. I want to know you better."

He patted the bed beside him. I was reminded how I used to try to get Josie, the cat, to sit on my lap. I hesitated, but I wanted to get to know him better also. What harm could there be in sitting closer to him?

I had stopped being aware of his scent in the way one gets used to an odor, whether it is good or bad, in a room. As I moved closer to him, that faint muskiness was fresh in my nostrils. I wondered if my breath was clean and, again, if I smelled of squash.

"I read *Romeo and Juliet* today," he said. "A fine story. I can see you are a romantic girl to like it so. Has there been romance in your life?"

I blushed and shook my head. It made me feel good that he appreciated my being romantic, where Simon thought it silly.

"You are not promised to anyone?"

I shook my head again. Girls of fifteen could be engaged, or even married, but such an early age was not common for women of my station.

"And you?"

It was a bold question, but I wanted to know. I knew women must run after any man so handsome.

"I am a good Puritan and would not trifle with a young woman."

I felt a swell of relief. It was something Patience had said, that he could be engaged or even married.

He asked me to tell him about my life in the castle.

I was lost, at first, but after a minute of awkwardness I found my tongue. I went on about how mother hated the castle, the cold stone and the hugeness, and how I loved those things. I told about all the things I loved: the library, the red brick in the afternoon light, the carvings all about, and going to the castle roof to look out over the fens. I told about Sarah's badness, Patience's friendship, and my father's temper.

John listened and nodded and smiled and told me about his sister.

"She is older now, but when she was younger she was very much like you."

He told me his father was a deacon in the church. John had gone to school and hoped to be a minister someday. He told me how sweet his sister was. She was younger than him but always looking out for him. She prepared the foods he liked best, especially a pie of pears, which was his favorite.

I thought that I would make him a pear pie, though then I recalled that pears would not ripen for a month or two.

We talked and talked about foods we liked and books we liked. I was excited to find that he, too, liked poetry. We quoted one or two poems we liked particularly. I told him about Milton. We had moved closer on the bed.

His smiling face took on a serious look.

"Today was such a fine day, even trapped inside this room. From my window, the sky was so blue and the clouds so white that I made up a poem of my own. For you. I have only the first two lines as yet.

*'Shall I compare thee to a summer's day?*
*Thou art more lovely and more temperate.'"*

He had written me a poem. I was moved. He put his arm around me. My back and shoulder, where his arm lay, felt hot. I knew I should pull away but I could not.

Perhaps if he had started by kissing me I would have been able to, but what he did was to raise my arm with his other hand—the one that wasn't around my shoulder—and begin to kiss away the squash soup on my wrist.

He smiled, and said that he could have dined off my arm. I laughed, and it took my fears away. His lips moved up my bare wrist and then over my shift and very gradually to my neck, which tingled in a way I had never felt.

Then he kissed me. His lips against mine were so soft that all my insides went molten. His arm moved further down my back and he drew me against his body, and his kiss became harder. I knew it was a sin, and I kept telling myself get up, leave now, but it was difficult when my whole body had melted. Finally, when his hands began to stray, I did manage to push myself away.

I was grateful that he did not press me, as my legs were trembling. If he had been insistent, I might not have been able to stand, let alone stand firm against him.

"There will be another day, sweet Anne. I will wait till tomorrow, something to look forward to during the long day."

I ran out of the room before I weakened. I could hardly breathe, the air felt so heavy in my chest. Every part of me was vibrating, and I longed to go back to him. I stumbled on the stairs again, stubbing my toe, and I did not even feel the pain until much later.

When I got to bed, Patience demanded to know what had happened; I had been gone so long, and she had been so worried. I would not tell her, and she became more and more upset. Finally I burst into tears, and she held me. I could not have said why I cried, but my feelings were so confused and intense there seemed no other way to express them. I think Patience guessed something of what had happened, without my saying, although she may have feared that even more had happened.

# Chapter Eleven

It seemed I had barely fallen asleep when the sun came up at five o'clock. It was time to get up to go to Boston for church. Never was one more in need of church and spiritual guidance than I, I thought. As I staggered out of bed, I noted the book of Milton's poems on the floor underneath and remembered that I had not finished reading Simon's paper.

I was so tired from lack of sleep, not only the night before but the previous nights, that I fell asleep immediately in the carriage. I woke with a start as we neared town. We were on a rise, and I could see the tower of our church, its bells calling us through the clatter of the horses.

There on the right was the gallows. It stood at the top of the rise, stark against the pale morning sky. Last year a thief had hung there. The image of his face, drawn back into a fearful smile, returned again and again in my dreams. I saw John's wondrous smile transformed into that image.

Much as my mind willed it away, that sight returned throughout the day as I tried to listen to Reverend Cotton. If John were caught, he would be hung. There was no question. If Father forced him to leave, he would be caught. Father would throw him out if he knew what we were doing in the secret room. We both would be punished.

Remembering the night before, I melted all over again. My knees went weak and I felt faint. I had found a poem in an old book in the library, mixed in with more religious poetry. I did not think Simon would have approved of it, but I loved it, and it was what kept going through my head. *Christ, if my love were in my arms and I in my bed again.* And then I saw the image of John's smile, transformed into the thief's smile, from the gallows.

THE FAIR WAS over now, and there was much less traffic into town. As we entered the market square, I spied the beggar man standing alone and watching our carriage. I looked away before he could catch my eye.

Entering the church, I took Sarah by the hand to be sure she did not run away. She had been surprisingly quiet that morning. She had let me sleep in the carriage, while it was her usual habit to kick or pinch me if I fell asleep. She was carrying a small purse, a nicety she usually disdains.

This day we planned to stay for afternoon services also, though it meant getting home very late. Now that the Earl was gone, Father's time was freer. At the noon break we went into the market square, unlike other Sundays when we ate with Reverend Cotton in his home, or someone else invited us to their house. Today there was no rain, though the sky had turned gray, so it was pleasant to walk around the square.

I checked the market posting board for notices about items for sale and events in Boston, and was glad I did not have to go to the eel-fishing contest to see who could catch the most eels, or the largest eel.

We had bread and cheese that Cook had packed for us, and we

went around to vendors to see what else they were offering. Sarah escaped from me for a time, and came back with a small treacle tart stuffed into her mouth.

When we returned for afternoon service, my mind was again caught in the wonder of the night before and fear of the consequences. I tried to think of what I should do this coming night. I prayed for guidance, but none came. I was afraid that once I saw John again and felt his smile, I would give in completely. Patience sat next to me, and I know she felt my turmoil.

She finally whispered in my ear, "Send me tonight."

It was the answer. I felt such relief. And terrible disappointment. I told myself it would give me time to compose myself, to think about what I truly wanted.

When we left the church, Father and Simon ahead of Mother and us girls as usual, there was a crowd—twenty or more—in the market place, and they seemed to be gathered about the posting board. We continued on toward our carriage without paying it much mind. Father does not like crowds, but I would have liked to see what was posted. At that moment, the old beggar in the rat-brown cloak appeared. He tried to get Father's attention, and Father brushed him aside. He then sidled up to me and grabbed me by my sleeve. I recoiled and thought how different the touch of a man on your arm could feel.

In a low voice the beggar man said, "Two things. First, for John Holland," and he handed me a piece of paper, which I pushed into my purse. "Second, you must listen. That notice on the board is about your family, and it means trouble for all of you."

I pushed forward to get to Father's side and repeated the message.

"Go see what it is," he said to Simon, but I pretended he meant me too.

The two of us raced off into the market square toward the posting board. Simon was faster, so I fell behind, but when we reached the crowd of people I pushed through more quickly, being smaller. Squeezing between a fat miller in a big white apron and a smelly man who must have been a tanner, I got close enough to see the board. On it, posted low, was the page Simon had addressed to me about religious tolerance and the error of the King's policies.

I could not believe it. It was as though some private dream, like the one about riding the horse on the fen, should have become written across the sky.

Sarah! It must have been she. The paper was attached right at the level she could reach. Who else would do such a thing? She was the only one who would not realize that to attack the King was treason.

What should I do? My name was on it. *Anne Dudley has asked a wicked question* … Everybody had already seen that, but it seemed better to take the paper. Perhaps no one would tell the Sheriff. I pulled it off and tucked it under my arm. The miller tried to stop me, but I wriggled out of his floury arms. I pushed back through the crowd. The miller cried, "Stop," but nobody thought he meant me, a young girl of no consequence. As I ran back across the marketplace toward our carriage, I saw one of the Sheriff's men in his red shirt approaching the board.

Simon ran beside me. "What was it? What was it?"

I showed him, as we hastened along. He turned pale when he saw it. He looked at me questioningly, and I said simply, "Sarah."

He nodded, and was completely silent for a while.

"Tell your father I will talk to him at the castle, and get everyone out of here as fast as you can," he said finally, as he veered off toward the stable where his horse was kept.

When I reached Father I was too afraid to speak. I handed him the paper and pointed behind me to the Sheriff's man sauntering toward the notice board.

"Hurry, we must hurry," I said.

Mother saw the urgency, if Father did not. She bustled us all, including Father, into the carriage and signaled to the driver to go fast. She might not have known what was happening but she knew how Father would attract attention to himself if he began to bellow.

Father was puzzling through the document.

He muttered, "What the Devil. Simon has written this piece of nonsense?"

When he was more than half-way through, at the part about the King, he exploded in a stream of curses unlike anything I had ever heard, including portions of God's anatomy that I was unsure about.

After several minutes, during which Mother had her ears covered and the rest of us sat like stone, he demanded to know what had happened.

I spoke, the words thick in my throat, explaining that Simon had given me this to read, and that I had hidden it under my bed within a book.

"And how did it wander into the Boston market?" he bellowed.

Nobody said anything for a while.

"It was posted low on the board," I said, finally.

"Sarah," he barked.

"Father, Anne is the bad girl, not me." Sarah spoke quickly. "She takes food from the table and says it is for you, and she is lying. She hides it under her bed. I followed her and I saw. This paper was hidden under her bed too. Mother will not listen to me about how bad she is. Anne gets up in the middle of the night and wanders about. She is up to something sinful. Nobody would listen to me. I thought if I put this up in the market, you and everyone would have to see how bad she is. It says Anne is wicked."

Sarah could read a little, but not well.

"Pull over!" Father yelled to the coachman.

Then he said to Sarah, "I am too angry to deal with you. I could hurt you."

I was surprised. I had never seen Father so angry, but he knew himself well enough to hold himself in check. He clambered over me and for the rest of the ride, almost three hours, he sat with the driver. Every few minutes we heard curses shouted to the sky.

It began to rain lightly and it felt cold, since we had dressed for fine weather. I shivered in the carriage, partly from cold and partly from fear. I found myself biting my fingers. I was worried what could happen to Simon for having written the piece, to Father, to John, to me in having to deal with Father's rage, and even to Sarah. From the things he was shouting, I thought if we had not feared we were being chased, Father might have stopped the carriage to beat Sarah and me. I wished Simon were with us so I could ask him what was going to happen.

We jostled along, faster than usual. Father kept urging haste on the coachman. None of us slept on this trip, and I noted every landmark: the little town of Kirkton, the bridge over the dikes. The gallows looked even more of an omen than it had on the way north.

We looked back at every bend in the road. Mother's face was pale and drawn, and Sarah had slunk into a corner of the carriage, too sullen to join in our fearful backward glances.

When we reached the tree-lined road that followed the river and led to Tattershall Castle, I breathed a sigh of relief. But as we rounded the next bend, we saw a cloud of dust far behind us. We all gasped at the same moment.

Father, on top of the carriage, yelled, "The pimpled Church of England swine. Get some speed out of the damned horses, Jack!"

I knew Father hoped to cross the moat and raise the drawbridge before the Sheriff's men caught up. It was no use. The carriage was no match for men on horses. The cloud of dust grew nearer and larger.

By the time we crossed the drawbridge, they were galloping alongside us. The Sheriff pulled ahead of us and signaled us to stop. I liked his fat, red face less than ever. We stopped in front of the castle.

"Stand down," the Sheriff said to Father.

The rest of us stepped out of the carriage as well. Mother and the other girls stood watching to see what would happen, but as more and more men on horses arrived, I slipped behind the others and began walking toward the castle. For once I was glad to be young and small for my age.

I could hear the beginning of the conversation behind me.

"An unfortunate document showed up today at the market in Boston. It was treasonous, and it was addressed to your daughter." Father replied, "Do you have it?"

I was so glad I had taken it away. Perhaps Father could talk his way out of it.

"In addition, it was written on the back of a statement of John Holland's treason. There is a rumor that he is here."

My hands were suddenly damp. The family might be saved from Sarah's folly, but Father would not be able to do anything to help John. It was up to me. The Sheriff's men had searched the castle before, but this time they would do it more thoroughly, and they would almost certainly find the secret room.

Think, think, I told myself frantically.

I headed toward the kitchen and could hear no more. Cook was reluctant to obey me. I had to command, in a voice I did not know I had. I sped back toward the castle with a bundle. I passed well away from my father and the group, but when the Sheriff shouted "Halt," I halted.

"Who goes?" he called.

I turned to face the Sheriff and the others and made a curtsey, as well as I could with my bundle.

"It is merely my eleven year old daughter," Father said. "I doubt she poses a threat."

"Was it you who removed the paper from the posting board?"

Oh Sarah, Sarah, show me how to lie. I smoothed my face and slowed my breath and said, "What paper, Sir?"

Father interrupted. "She is only a child, and a little simple besides."

The Sheriff shrugged and made a motion with his hand toward the door.

I walked into the castle in the manner of a young, embarrassed girl. I did not think of it till later, but Father himself knew how to lie; it had been four years since I was eleven. I ran up the stairs to the second floor.

When I got to the fireplace, there were two servants standing in front of it, so deep in conversation they did not hear me. I heard the word "Sheriff." They looked up at me with guilty expressions.

"If you go to the window there, you can hear them," I said.

They looked surprised that I had not reprimanded them for gossip. They hastened across the room toward the window and were quickly absorbed in the scene outside.

I pulled the rabbit ears and hurried under the tapestry. In a moment, I was inside the secret room.

John had his knife poised to attack as I entered. He dropped his arm when he saw it was I. His window faced away from the courtyard, but he must have heard the servants talking, to be so prepared.

"Hurry," I said, handing him my bundle. Again I was surprised by the level of command in my voice.

He swore and grumbled but he obeyed me, and in a few moments we slipped from the room.

The servants had their heads out the window and one of them gasped, "They're coming towards the castle."

# Chapter Twelve

We ran down the stairs, John pulling me so that I slid around the corner. We reached the open front door just as the Sheriff's men approached. They were perhaps ten feet away.

"Slow down," I said. I took a deep breath, went out the door, and made a curtsey to the men. Then we walked sharply to the right, down toward the moat.

"Hold," one of the men said loudly. "Who goes there?"

"I am the Steward's daughter, helping the cook. We are going to pick dandelion greens for the evening meal."

I hoped that they would see a young girl and a tall cook wearing the bonnet and apron that I had forced Cook to give me. John's long hair peeked out from under the bonnet.

The Sheriff's man waved us away, and John and I tried not to hurry toward the water.

"We must pick for a while," I said. One of the men stayed at the door, looking out over the castle grounds. Bent over, we began to pluck leaves and stretched out our aprons to put them in.

"Is this a dandelion?" he asked.

"No, that's a mullion. Dandelions have broader leaves."

"I do know dandelions, just not the plant without the flower."
He seemed cross, perhaps because he was as afraid as I was. My
mouth was dry.

John kept glancing over to the moat, and finally he spied what I
had told him about while he put on Cook's great white skirt in the
castle. Sam's little boat lay half hidden in the reeds. It could not be
seen from the castle. John could get into it and escape.

We kept glancing back at the castle, and finally saw another of
the Sheriff's men come out of the castle and engage the sentry in
conversation.

We moved slowly, picking all the way to the very edge of the
moat.

I muttered to John, "You must take the first, left fork. You could
miss it, it is small and heads off at an angle. There is a big egret's nest
in a tree to the north as a landmark."

"An egret's nest?" He snorted. "I do not know an egret's nest from
a wren's. You must come, and once I find the turn, I can put you off."

"I have only been there once," I said. It had been three years
ago, when Sam had taken me eeling with him. I dropped into the
boat after John.

It was small, about seven feet long and a foot and a half wide,
with a flat bottom. There were no oars, just a pole that Sam used to
propel himself, and a smaller pole that I could perhaps use. John and
I barely fit, but there was no time for niceties. I wished I were not
wearing my Sunday dress with the wide skirt and was glad I had shed
some petticoats. Church in Boston this morning seemed long ago.

"We should take this inlet into the fens. Then we need not go
around the bend where we will be visible at the drawbridge," I said,
and John nodded. There was a red-coated sentry stationed at the
drawbridge, who would surely not let us leave the castle if he saw us.

We cut into the passage, barely wide enough for the tiny boat
to get through. Reeds brushed our faces.

"What will happen when they realize we are gone? Perhaps we should simply have hidden you in an outbuilding until they left."

"No, it is not safe for me here any longer. They will find the secret room and they will station someone at the castle. The servants would talk if there was a strange person in the outbuildings."

John was having a hard time poling, as reeds caught the boat on either side and the depth of the water was only a couple of feet. The sweat began to bead on his forehead as he pushed us along. The reeds were above our heads now. We could only see the upper stories of the castle. If someone was posted at the top they could see us, but not well. Soon we would disappear from sight altogether.

I faced forward, straining to see where the channel might open up. Flies and mosquitoes swarmed around us and began to feast. Our skirts covered our legs, and my shift protected my chest and upper arms. I had a kerchief tied round my shoulders. I took off my bonnet, draped the kerchief around my face so only my eyes showed, and retied the bonnet. My flaxen blue skirt, cleaned after I had gotten it so dirty at the fair, was now filthy on the bottom, and I wondered how I would look when I returned to the castle. I almost laughed, realizing that I had no idea at all of what would happen to us. Worrying about my clothes seemed to belong to another lifetime.

I remembered the beggar man's message for John and handed it to him.

He read it and laughed. "Good," he said. He says that there is a boat heading towards Holland tomorrow, and that he will wait for me along the river today and tomorrow. Also that the Sheriff's men are looking for me. I would have had to leave today anyway, even if the Sheriff had not arrived when he did."

"Who is this beggar?"

"Who knows. He is a rebel against the King, he is a Puritan, he is a scoundrel."

"That is no answer."

76

John sighed. "I will tell you all I know. First, do we have anything to eat?"

I realized that John had not eaten all day, while I had taken a good midday meal in Boston. I was hungry myself, now that I was a bit more relaxed. It was probably past nine o'clock, and the midsummer sun was finally beginning to set.

I pointed to the dandelions he had dumped from his apron into the bottom of the boat. He made a face.

"Speaking of beggars, they cannot…" I said, and he nodded, knowing the end of the expression.

I added the dandelions from my own apron, dipped a few into the water to wash the dirt from them, then handed them to John. I ate a few myself. Dandelions are so bitter before they've been cooked. We ate them slowly and we ate them all.

While we were munching, John told me about the beggar man.

"He comes from Scotland, originally, but has lived in these parts many years. He goes back and forth, from here to Holland, taking Puritans who seek to escape, and bringing goods back and forth for those who have made the trip. I think he takes a good cut for his labors."

"He seemed so ragged."

"That filthy cloak is a disguise. He does not want to attract attention."

I digested that. I seemed to be learning a lot about lying, today. People were not always what they seemed.

I wanted to tell John to go faster, to leave some of the insects behind, as well as to escape, but I realized he was going as fast as he could. I picked up the small pole in the bottom of the boat and began to help.

We had poled for perhaps ten minutes, the channel growing narrower, then wider, and then narrower again, nothing but reeds and insects. Flies, big green ones and little, blue damselflies, buzzed about catching an occasional mosquito. Even in our dangerous situation I watched the damselflies, so bright they seemed to have swallowed a piece of the sun.

We came to a channel that crossed our path. There were only a few trees, and none with an egret's nest. I thought we should take the path anyway. It seemed to me to be the right distance from the castle.

John said, "No, this is so narrow we would not be able to pass. It cannot be the right channel. We must press on."

My arms grew tired, and I rested for longer and longer periods. John was cursing under his breath more frequently. He had placed Cook's apron around his face to keep off the bugs. He looked alarming, and then I thought I must look quite strange myself.

I picked up the little pole again, and pushed it into the water. I almost fell out of the boat and I almost lost the pole. There was no bottom here that I could reach. We were in a deeper channel.

Then the passage widened. There was another cross channel, wider still than the one we were on.

We turned in what we decided was the direction of Boston. There was a small current in that direction, so that John did not need to pole. Indeed, for a short period, his pole did not touch the bottom.

My heart lifted. The bugs were left behind, since we were further away from the grasses, and it felt like we were making headway. We were actually going to get away.

I remembered that John was supposed to put me ashore, once we reached the channel. We were so much further away from the castle than I had thought we would be, however, and I had no idea of how to get back. Also, there were only reeds and more reeds, no firm ground on which to let me off.

I heard the church clock from far away, striking ten bells. A great deal had happened since I rose at five that morning, and I was exhausted. I had to sleep, even though there was so little room in the boat. The back of my clothes would be wet and muddy, but I lay down and was asleep in an instant.

I woke to the sound of cursing, and with some sharp pains as bugs bit me. It was dark now, but I could see by the faint light of a half moon that we were stuck, surrounded by reeds. The channel had petered out.

# CHAPTER THIRTEEN

"WHAT SHALL WE do now?" I was groggy from sleep, but it took only a moment to realize our danger.

"God's teeth, this has been an accursed trip if ever there was one."

John went on, with worse than that. I felt somehow to blame, as though my plan had not been a good one. I bit my tongue. He was with me; that made a difference, didn't it?

"Were there other turn offs besides that one at the beginning?" I asked.

John shook his head violently, while a steady stream of curses still emerged from his mouth.

"It is so very far." My voice sounded thin to my ears. "What if the Sheriff's men are around? We must go back now, while it is still dark." I answered my own question.

John had already turned the punt around and was poling back, struggling. I was able to help with the little pole for a time, until the channel deepened. The evening star had moved quite a ways across the sky, and I estimated I had slept an hour or so. I was still exhausted, and I could not have continued poling even if I were able to reach the bottom.

"I can put you off at the castle," John said, after a bit.

We had not talked about what I would do. We had not talked much at all. After the night before, so long ago, when words came rolling off my tongue and his as well, it felt odd. Here I was with a strange man in the middle of the night. Most of the men in the county would never marry me now, assuming that a man and a woman could not be in such a situation without intimacy. All day at church I had thought about intimacy, and now that we were alone it had not crossed my mind. Danger drove away softer thoughts, I supposed. And talking about books and food we liked seemed silly at the moment.

I wished I had not got into the boat, and I wished John had taken the first channel that I wanted to take. I did not say these things.

When we had briefly talked of plans, it had been to get John to Boston. What would happen to me was not a part of the plan. I could not go with John unless he married me, and he had not suggested that.

As I reached that point in my thoughts, during the long silence between us, John said, "You cannot go with me except as man and wife, and I am not ready for that. I need to be free in order to escape onto a boat and go to Holland, and then to the New World."

I said nothing. I did not want to go to the New World. I would have liked him to want me to come.

"I did . . . I do care about you, little one."

"It is night now, the summer day is over," I said.

"What are you talking about?"

"Your poem. You compared me to a summer's day. On a punt lost in the middle of the fens in the middle of the night, we are far from that summer's day." I was not quite sure what I meant.

We said nothing further for a time. Then he said again, "We will go back to the castle and I will set you out."

It did seem the best idea. Not a good plan, but the only plan. We rode in silence, except for the sounds of John poling and cursing under his breath. I helped when the boat came near to the shore. Finally we came back to the point where the current was strong. Before it had helped us, now it was almost impossible to move against it. I tried to use my little pole as an oar, but it hardly made a difference. John swore again, and even in the dark I could see the sweat on his brow and his clothes. It was a good thing the night was warm, because he was as wet as though he had bathed in the stream with his clothes on.

My mind kept going back to our conversation, though we said nothing more. I felt regret that he had not asked me to marry him. I also had a small feeling, in the back of my mind, that if he had asked me I would have had to answer, and I did not know what I would have said. It was partly my fear of the wolves and bears and Indians in the New World, but also partly that I did not know if I wanted to be with him, John, the person he was.

And why not? What was it? That he was swearing so mightily? My father swore worse than the townspeople, and I loved him anyway. Perhaps it was that John had never in any way praised the way I had smuggled him out of the castle and into the boat. Something silly like that. Why had he told me get into the boat with him? He was the older one, the one who should have had better judgment.

I could see the castle tower in the distance, with the moon behind it. We passed the narrow turning that John would need to take to get to Boston. John put his finger to his lips, then gestured with his hand over his eyes for me to keep watch for the Sheriff's men. I strained through the dark as we grew nearer to the moat.


"THERE HE IS!"

I could not see the man who had screamed. My heart began to pound in my chest. My hands felt as wet as John's.

John began to pole furiously, away from the castle, and I began, also frantically, pushing away, away, as fast as ever we could.

An explosion rocked the boat. We had been hit. We heard another, then another huge noise, and finally our boat turned into the little channel, the narrow one that John had rejected the first time. We were out of view.

John let out a gasp of relief, and I began a silent prayer of thanksgiving.

"Are you all right?" he asked.

"Yes, and you?"

"I have a pain in my shoulder."

The dim light of the moon showed a black splotch against the white of his shift.

"Shall we bind it?

"Not now, we must get further away. They could follow."

The boat seemed all right, or at least it kept floating. We continued rafting. I felt fairly safe. The fens were so easy to hide in. If the Sheriff's men caught up with us, all we had to do was get out of the boat and kneel in the reeds. Nobody would find us unless they tripped over us.

It was then we heard the dogs.

# Chapter Fourteen

I KNEW IT could be all over. If the dogs had our scent they would follow to the ends of the earth, yipping and yelping, and we would be caught for certain.

I poled like a madwoman. I glanced up for a moment and saw John grimace with pain while he poled and poled.

I supposed it was the Earl's dogs the Sheriff had taken, since he had none with him when he arrived. Father and Simon sometimes hunted with the Earl, but I never had. Hunting was not to my taste. I liked dogs, but not these. They never wanted to play or be petted.

The barking was louder. I could see the water moving behind us, and the dark, round shape of heads. They were coming.

John managed to gasp, between strokes, "Smash them on the head with your pole if they catch up."

I grunted. I did not know how well I could smash a dog, I was so frightened. John moaned between each rise and fall of the pole.

The narrow passage was hard going, but then it began to widen just a bit. All at once it seemed as though our boat were a seed and the stream were a person who spat that seed away. We were flung into a wider river and were moving very fast.

"Thank you, Lord!" I breathed, and tears of relief began to run down my face.

John had collapsed onto the boat. I crawled forward toward him. The boat was unsteady in the current, going whichever way the river wanted, so it was hard to move. At one point I was almost flung off into the depths. I wished I knew how to swim. Finally I reached John, lying motionless. The black splotch on his shirt had widened, and now that I could see more clearly, I found it reddish black and hard to my touch.

I began to pull up his shift to take it off. A thought flashed through my mind about how intimate the action was, and yet not at all intimate. He groaned. I took hold of the shoulder seam, one hand on either side, and prayed his seamstress had been careless and made big stitches. I had to use my teeth, but the seam gave way, exposing his shoulder. He groaned again as the fabric ripped, and the dried blood also tore. But the wound was seeping anyway.

I had to shut my eyes for a moment. Even in the dark, I could see how much blood he had lost. It was everywhere. Dried blood and fresh oozing blood. The ball of the musket had shot through cruelly, leaving rough edges and black gunpowder marks around it.

I had once seen Father bind up a farmer's wounds after an accident with a scythe. While he did it, he had launched into a story about his war experience and dealing with men who were dying of their wounds. The important thing was to make the bleeding stop.

I looked at what I had. My kerchief was too soft, and the silk of my dress not strong enough, and the linen of my apron too stiff. I pulled my skirt up a bit and began to rip at the soft linen of my shift. I had to use my teeth to get the rip started. I thought that lifting my skirt, as I was, in front of a man, was not like what I had imagined. I was tearing strips of my shift about three inches across. Each time I got to the side seam I had to use my teeth again. One of my fingernails ripped. My shift was getting shorter and shorter.

Then, when I had the strips, I began to bind. Each strip barely reached around his shoulder, and there was only a little of the fabric left to tie. I knew I had to make the binding very tight.

It was painstaking work. John groaned in pain each time I touched him, and tears of frustration sprang to my eyes. The first bandages became completely bloody in an instant.

"You must lie completely still." I wished I had St. John's Wort to reduce the bleeding.

We were speeding along the river, the little raft bouncing up and down with the current. We were in the river's power. John was spent. Even if I tried to use his pole, I would not be able to control it.

John lay on the bottom of the boat, and I sat beside him watching the banks fly by, black in the darkness against the lighter water. Each time the boat jumped through the current, John moaned.

We went for ages, it seemed. The river continued to widen. Finally the current slowed, we began to move at a calmer pace, and John's moans stopped.

There was a dim light in the east. The banks of the river began to take on their rich brown color, and I could see the red of John's spilled blood clearly. A bird or two began to sing.


THIS WAS A new day. I had spent the night alone with a man. Nothing had happened and a great deal had happened.

And then I saw a figure, ahead, on a bend in the river.

"Ahoy," the person called.

Squinting, I could see it was the beggar man.

I took up the big pole and pushed it down as far as I could. It touched the bottom, and I was able to direct it a little bit. Twice more, and we were going to make land.

"Well done!" the beggar man shouted as we hit the bank. He grabbed the edge of the boat and began to drag it ashore.

"Of course, the current carries boats in here, it is why I chose this place," he said, as I climbed off. I felt unsteady on my feet after being on a boat so long.

"And what have we here? God's eyeballs."

He looked at John, lying pale and bloody in the bottom of the boat, then climbed in himself. He checked my bandaging and grunted, "Not bad. He will live."

Together we tightened two of the strips. It was so much easier, with one person to hold the strip tight and the other to tie it.

We had barely finished when the beggar said, "We must be off. A packet leaves for Holland this evening."

"What about her?" John asked.

"You have come a long way on the river but, as the crow flies, you are not so far from the castle. The road is a quarter mile away." He pointed away from the sun, now higher in the sky. "It is then only a two or three mile walk back to Tattershall."

"Leave her here, you mean."

I did not like being talked about as though I were not there.

"Yes," the beggar man said.

I felt a pang of fear in my stomach. "And what if the Sheriff's men are still around?" I asked.

"It is John they want, not you. You are the Earl's Steward's daughter. You will be safe."

I was not convinced. I had helped John escape, and my blue dress, covered with dirt and dampness, would tell anyone that I had been on an escapade. The Earl was in prison, and there was no guarantee for the Earl's Steward's daughter.

"No time. We must be off. Should I turn away while you say your good-byes?" His laugh was wicked.

I blushed.

John seemed to turn a paler shade. "Come here," he said, and I walked to the boat.

He reached his hand to me. I took it. It was warm and red, and my heart moved as I saw and felt the blisters, broken and bloody.

He lifted my hand to his lips. "I am sorry, my sweet." He spoke low, so the beggar man could not hear. "My loving thoughts go with you."

I could not make a reply, so many feelings and thoughts rose up in me. Love for him. Longing. Anger that he would leave me, leave me like this in the middle of the fens, and fear for both of us.

When John released my hand, the beggar man pushed the boat off, climbed aboard, and picked up the pole.

"That way." He pointed again for me, and they were gone down the river.

I did not immediately take his direction. I relieved myself, something I had needed to do for some time. I was horridly hungry and thirsty. I washed my face and hands at the river bank and scooped up water to drink from my hand. I knew that drinking water was dangerous, but this was an emergency, and there was certainly no ale or cider or milk about.

I looked for berries by the river and found a few green ones. They did little for my hunger. I thought that the beggar man had probably been carrying food, and felt new anger that he had not shared any with me.

Who had saved John from the Sheriff's men? And had bound his wounds and saved his life? The Earl's Steward's daughter. Me. The one who now had to make her way back to the castle alone, without food or help of any kind. I thought of how my family saw me as frail and sickly, and how neither John, nor the beggar man, nor the Sheriff's men saw me that way at all.

The thought brought a smile to my face. I would get back to the castle alone, I would.

# Chapter Fifteen

I headed in the direction the beggar man had pointed. It was slow going, as the ground was so marshy. I was up to my ankles in dirty water. With each step the mud held onto my shoes, and I had to pull them out, tensing my toes to keep the shoes on my feet. I shivered in the cool morning. Mosquitoes swarmed over me, and I covered my head with my apron. I kept looking around for the road, and finally—it seemed forever—there it was. I thanked the Lord and set out to the left, pleased that I would soon be home.

It must have been about six o'clock in the morning when I reached the road. It was too far from the castle to hear the church bell, so I judged by the light. It had reached full light, June being that time of year when there were only a few hours of real night. It was not far to the castle, but it was dangerous. Robbers were common and there were other dangers to a woman walking alone. I hoped I would not meet anyone.

I hurried along as fast as I could, which helped warm me and stopped the shivering. The morning sun began to dry my dress and shoes. The insects buzzed along behind me, but if I walked fast I had a little peace from them. I would not say it was pleasant, but it was better than being in the marsh.

I kept looking into the distance, ready to step off the path and hide in the reeds if anyone came. Closer and closer I came to the castle, my heart lighter and lighter. Finally, I was only a quarter mile or so from the village that surrounded the castle, and I relaxed. From here, I could run into the village if anyone accosted me. Of course there were still the Sheriff's men to watch for. Perhaps they would have left, but I had to plan for the possibility that they were still watching for John and me.

I thought about how I could enter the village unseen. There was only one path in. The village had been constructed to be surrounded by open space, so that any intruder would stand out. If I stayed on the road I would be visible for a long way. I decided to work my way around through the marshes, so I could hide in them if I needed to. The closest house to the fens, in the village, was Davey the baker's, and I would head for that.

I could smell the fires of the villagers and, faintly, the bread cooking at the bakery. Saliva filled my mouth. I was so hungry. I planned to go just around the next corner, still out of sight of the village, and then step into the fens. As I rounded the corner, I saw the red shirt of a Sheriff's man.

Had he seen me? I shrank back behind a tree and stood motionless. He let out a shout and began to run in my direction, along the road.

I turned and ran back around the bend and into the fens, plunging through the reeds, again up to my ankles in muck. My shoes were gone in an instant. I was perhaps a hundred feet from the road. Soon the Sheriff's men would come around the corner and see me, if I were standing, so I lay down. The reeds would hide me, and if the men tried to blunder through them, they would still be unlikely to find me. As long as they did not have the dogs...

I could hear the men, now, calling to each other. There were three or four distinct voices, but no barking.

"I'll run back along the road. If she went back, I can catch up with her quickly—I know I can run faster than a wench. You stay here and go through the fens. She probably went to ground."

A groan. I could hear slogging sounds, as boots were sucked by mud. Some voices were louder, some grew more distant.

"We must punish her before we take her back, for making us get so foul."

There was a laugh.

Every exposed part of my face and arms was covered with mosquitoes, and I could do nothing to slap at them for fear of making noise. I lay on my belly, one arm over my head and the other under it, to keep my face clear. I was slowly sinking deeper. I reminded myself that there was no quicksand at this part of the fens, but as I felt myself sink, I panicked, and almost began struggling to get out—the worst thing to do.

Trust God, I thought, and I let my body go as it chose. My dress was so heavy, now, with water and mud, that it seemed like a person in the swamp was pulling me down. I told myself that at least no blue showed from my dress to catch their attention. Soon I was holding onto reeds to keep myself from going under.

The voices came nearer and nearer, until I could see the boots of a man about twenty feet away.

I took a breath and lowered my head, pushing it under the foul water. I held my breath as long as I could, and when it felt like I would burst, raised my head slowly. The boots were no longer visible. I wiped my face against my arm, to get enough mud off so I could breathe.

The voices sounded further away, and soon I could no longer hear them. What should I do now? What if they had left someone to watch for me? But it might be my only chance to evade them. It would be safer to wait till night, but could I stay here that long? I heard the church bell ring nine as I lay there, uncertain.

My view of the world now was the mud, and the lower part of four or five reeds sticking into it. I watched as three new mosquitoes landed upon the reeds. Then I felt something bumping against me in the ooze. Eels, probably. I made up my mind. I could not stay there all day.

It took me a long time to pull myself out of the sucking mud. I looked around and did not see anyone. I surveyed myself. I had no shoes, and I was black from head to foot. Slime dripped from my hair. My dress was so heavy I could hardly move, and when I did put one foot in front of the other, the movement caused mud to fall.

I shook myself like a dog, shutting my eyes and feeling clods fly in all directions. I dipped my hands in the dirty water and tried to wipe my face. That was all I had time for.

I made a prayer and started out. I could not chance the road, in case someone was watching. I might still be seen in the fen, but I could escape more easily. Slogging through the reeds was slow and painful, especially since my shoes were gone. I held back a moan with almost every step, as the harsh plants cut my feet. I tried to avoid them but it was almost impossible. When there were open places, I sank to my ankles, sometimes to the middle of my calves, and had to pull my leg out. The reeds got under my skirts, as well, and cut my legs. It was easier to walk if I lifted my petticoats, and I resigned myself to more cuts.

It was not far to the castle, but I was moving so slowly. I could see the road from where I was, and I kept a constant watch on it for the Sheriff's men. At any moment one of them could appear.

And then I did see a figure approaching on the road. I could feel my palms grow sweaty as I fell to my knees into the reeds. Then I saw. It was Simon.

I almost shrieked with joy. Simon! I caught myself in time. I hurried toward the road, not noting anymore how badly I cut my feet. I waved wildly, and as I got nearer he saw me. He stopped, looking at the black apparition. I tried to wipe the mud off my face, pointed and gestured who knows what, and finally I saw him give a start of recognition.

He began to run toward me till he hit the marsh. He put his finger to his lips, and I knew he wanted to shout as well. The mud hindered us both, but the moment came when he caught me in his arms.

I began to sob uncontrollably. I was safe.

# CHAPTER SIXTEEN

OF COURSE I was not safe. Now we both had to evade the Sheriff's men. But I was no longer alone. He picked me up, carrying me in his arms as he stumbled through the grasses. He, too, was avoiding the road.

He kept murmuring, "Oh little one, how good it is to see you. I have been searching and searching for you, and now you are here."

I told him all that had happened, and he just held me tighter and murmured more.

He told me that the Sheriff's men had discovered the secret room. John had put Cook's clothes on over his pants but he had left some other clothes of his own in the room. And they had found some extra petticoats I had shed. Then one of the Sheriff's men remembered how a girl and the cook had walked past them, and he called the alarm.

I was so relieved that Simon had not been arrested. Father had argued that it was hearsay to arrest a man without any proof of what he had written. The Sheriff's man had not read the statement, and most of the townsfolk gathered around the market notice board did not read well enough to be good witnesses.

SIMON TOOK ME into the castle village, just as I would have gone myself, toward Davey the baker's. There was no one around and he hustled me inside. Davey's dark head and broad shoulders were bent in front of the oven as he took out a loaf on the long wooden paddle. He looked up, his eyes puzzled. Not a customer, but two muddy folk, one of them unrecognizable. He was not too astonished to put the loaf down carefully on the counter. Then he came out from behind and spoke to Simon.

"What on God's earth?"

"It is too long to explain, but the Sheriff's men are looking for Anne."

"That is Anne?" He stared at me and then his face changed. "Hell's bells."

"Can you hold her here till nightfall? I will come back for her then and sneak her into the castle."

Davey did not speak.

"If she is discovered, it will go hard on the Earl and everyone at the castle."

I was glad to have Simon with me, to persuade Davey.

"Of course I want no trouble for the family," Davey said slowly, "but I must think of myself as well."

"If she is found, I will say I ordered you at the Steward's command."

Davey nodded.

Simon said, "Take care of her, Davey," and to me, "I shall see you at nightfall. Have no fear."

He swallowed hard. He walked out and I felt alone again. Even with Davey there, I could not help but be afraid.

Davey gestured for me to come into the back of the store where his living quarters were. They were plain: a bed, two stools, and a small table. I could see that someone had tried to make it cheerful. A piece of pretty striped wool hung on the wall, as well as an old picture of Queen Elizabeth that many common people still had. The back of the bread oven stuck into the room, which must have been wonderful in winter and dreadful in the heat of summer. For me, still wet and chilled, it felt lovely. I realized I had been shivering ever since I got out of the fen.

Davey sat me on a stool. "What shall I do with you?"

"Oh, something to eat—please, please."

In spite of the fear and the shivering and the mud, what I wanted most was a piece of the loaf Davey had taken from the oven. He went into the shop and came back with half the loaf and a lump of butter. As I spread the butter on the bread, it melted into the holes and crevices. It tasted better than anything I had ever eaten, though there was a bit of grit in it from the dirt on my hands. I ate every crumb, and the glass of milk he brought, as well.

Next, Davey brought me a bowl of water and a cloth. I laughed, as I did not know where to begin. Then he laughed as well. Then I laughed because I was laughing and it had been so long since I had laughed. And then Davey laughed harder, because laughter spreads like oil on water.

"Have you any other clothes?" I asked, when we had stopped. I needed to change out of my clothes and put on clean dry ones.

He looked hard at me.

"You know Joan died of the pox only three months ago. I have not been able to give her things away, and in fact I do not want to. It gives me some comfort to see them hanging on the hook as they always did. I could let you wear them, I suppose."

I was aware, then, that he was a young man, and I a young woman. I think he felt uncomfortable about that too, for he said, "It is not seemly for you to be in my house alone. It is less seemly for you to undress in my house."

"What is seemly does not matter to me. Thank you for your care, and I will see my father thanks you also."

I had come a long way. Two days before I would not have said these words, but I had spent the night alone with a young man in a boat, and what I thought seemly had changed a great deal.

He brought me his wife's old clothes, carefully laying each garment on the bed as though it had belonged to a queen. There was an old shift, a skirt of faded blue linen to wear over it, and a bonnet of the same fabric, even more faded. Joan had been pretty, with blond curls and lovely skin, and I wondered how pretty she might have been had she worn Arbella's clothes. We had all grieved when the pox had taken Joan as well as several others in the village. Those it left alive had been marked with horrid pock marks on the face. Marianne had been the exception. She had been sick, but not badly, and her face had healed miraculously.

Davey retreated to the front room. I washed my face as well as I could in the basin. The water was black by then, but I bent my head and dipped my hair in. When I drew it up my hair still felt stiff and dirty. I wanted a bath, but it was a beginning. Then I took off my clothes. Though I had dripped so much mud, it had caked, and my dress stood by itself when I put it on the floor.

I lifted up the dry shift Davey had left for me. It was gray and worn, with the edges around the neck all fringed and the seam on the side beginning to unravel. I slipped it on and felt warmer immediately. The skirt was so thin, from use and washings, that I could see the light through it.

I had the strange sensation of becoming another person, like I had as a child dressed up in my mother's clothes. This time I was a village wife who worked hard each day pulling loaves from the fiery oven, red in the face. A woman who had only bread to eat, never had children, and died before her time.

I was not going to die before my time if I could help it.

What to do with my clothes? They were full of rips, and washing would never remove the dirt. I wondered if Marianne would want them, then laughed to myself. They were unmendable. The fabric was too fine for rags. I was so trained not to throw things away that I walked around the dress to see if there was any part that could be saved. Then it occurred to me, what if the Sheriff's men came looking through the village for me when they did not find me in the fens? If they discovered my clothes, I would be caught for certain.

I gathered the dirty shift and dress into a ball. After glancing out to be certain that Davey had no customers, I brought the clothes to him and asked him to put them on the fire. He looked unwilling, thinking no doubt of what they had cost.

When I said, "What if the Sheriff's men come looking for me?" he opened the oven door and threw in the clothes.

"If they do come in, I am your wife. They are not from around here and they will not know about Joan," I said.

He nodded, and I returned to the living space.

The burning linen and silk stank for awhile, even in the back room. I was still cold, so I took a blanket from the bed to wrap around myself. I pulled the stool as close to the back of the oven as I could, and eventually my shivering stopped.

I was very tired, having gone without sleep for two days except for an hour in the boat. I lay down on the bed under the blanket, Joan's bonnet still on, and fell asleep immediately. I dreamed I was still out on the water swaying up and down, only my parents were there, and I was explaining to them how to pole the boat.

I woke with a start to a loud bang, which I thought in my dream was a gun shot. It was, in fact, the sound of the front door being flung open, smashing against the wall. I heard loud, demanding voices and realized it was the Sheriff's men.

Frantic, I thought of hiding, but it was too late. They were coming into the room. I pulled Joan's bonnet over my forehead, and put my hand to my face.

"It is my wife," Davey was saying. "She is sick."

Three large men filled the room. They were muddy and angry. Their faces were not familiar; there were none that I had seen on the stairs when I left the castle. My heart was beating fast, and I could feel the bread and butter in my stomach threaten to come up. My face was flushed from sleep and the heat of the room.

"How do we know it is your wife? She looks young. It could be the girl."

"Would the Steward's daughter lie in my bed?" Davey asked.

Years of being sickly had taught me how to act. I moaned a little, used the side of my hand to wipe at my cheek, and said in a weak voice, "Oh, Davey, I hope it is not the pox."

They left quickly then. My heart gradually slowed down, and I gave another prayer of thanks.

Davey came back in the room, his face pale. "That were a bit close."

"Thank goodness I was so tired and fell asleep."

I started to thank him for what he was risking, his life probably, and I could not find the words. I had to swallow, so as not to cry. He understood, I think, because he left the room right away, as if feeling awkward.

The rest of the day passed as I fell in and out of sleep. One of the Sheriff's men did come back to order a loaf of bread, and fortunately I was again lying on the bed rather than out in the front of the shop.

We ate again in the evening; more bread, this time with a bit of cheese. I was grateful, and the fresh warm bread still tasted delicious. I missed the kind of meal we had in the castle, with meat and vegetables. I knew that ordinary people did not have such meals, of course, but I had never spent a day like this in a villager's house. Davey was doing his best for me, pulling out a bottle of cider like the ones we drank at the castle. It had dust upon it, having been saved for a special occasion.

I asked Davey more about his wife. "She was beautiful," I said.

"Yes. She helped me with the baking, and we had many loving times. That is not what I miss most about her. What comes to my mind, always, is the way she used to sing. All day long she would hum, like a small, happy bird. The days are silent now."

I had a sudden thought of John. Would he feel that way about me, missing me? I was certain he would not. And what did I miss of him? What came to mind was his blistered hands, the way they had felt in mine. I would always hold that moment.

As the evening wore on I became impatient. I could sleep no more. I wanted to be home. How would I get into the castle? First I would have to get across the moat, I knew not how. The Sheriff would be bound to have posted someone there. And there was only one entrance to the castle, right in front for all to see.

# CHAPTER SEVENTEEN

As I lay on the bed, wide awake, I heard the door of the bakery open and a voice I recognized as Simon's. I felt myself smiling from the pleasure of it.

I jumped up. I ran to the front of the store to embrace him again as I had in the fens, then stopped, suddenly shy. He looked into my eyes, then away, and I wondered if he felt shy also. I had never before felt shy with Simon.

"Did you tell them all I was here? Are they angry?" I feared Father's anger especially.

"No, they are all relieved and excited. Your father wanted to come as well, but I would not hear of it. He did provide the rope for you to crawl up, on the way in."

"Where is it?"

"I have already tied it to the window frame in the back."

I smiled again. "Just what I was thinking." It was how Sam got in and out of the castle at night.

"And your father has reminded me several times of the siege of Amiens."

I had thought of that, as well, but saw no way to apply it to our own situation. When I pressed Simon, he said that I would see.

We took leave of Davey, who finally accepted the pound note that Simon kept pressing into his hand. It was probably as much as Davey made in a month.

It was black outside. Clouds covered the moon that had lit our way through the channels of the fens the night before. We walked in silence, in the direction of the gate house.

"How did you get out?" I whispered.

"I told the Sheriff's man who is on guard there that I could not sleep, that I was going for a walk."

We went on a bit further. Joan's shoes were too big for my feet and kept slipping off. Just like walking through the fens, I had to tense my toes to keep them on. I could not restrain myself from asking, in a tiny voice, "So where is your bag of walnuts?"

"No, I have better. I have a bag of money."

I was so pleased with the idea that I uttered an exclamation.

"Hush. It is still difficult. You must be quick and quiet as a cat stalking its prey, or we will both be arrested."

I could see the guardhouse by the drawbridge, faintly silhouetted against the clouds, and there was an even fainter figure in front of it. When we were close enough to see the figure move, we knew we could be seen as well, especially me in my pale dress. I dropped to my knees to crawl the remaining way. Simon stopped to wait for me to get to the guardhouse. Joan's dress was much less bulky than my own had been, but it was still hard to move in it. Impatient, I pulled it up around my waist and crawled on my bare knees, regardless of what Simon might think of me for not being ladylike. I tried to imagine myself a cat, slinking towards a mouse. It helped me control my breathing, which was loud and fast.

As I came within a hundred yards, the Sheriff's man went into the guardhouse, and I gave another of those thanks to God. I scurried on my knees as fast as I could and stationed myself against the side of the guardhouse, at the base of the moat. I could hear the guard inside moving around restlessly, cursing, sighing with boredom.

I watched Simon approach and knew he could see me by the side of the house. I tried to keep completely silent. My breath still seemed so loud that I feared the guard would hear it.

"Halt, who goes there?" the Sheriff's man yelled, and he ran from the guard house. My heart almost stopped, as I thought he had heard me.

"Only me," Simon called.

The guard grunted. I crouched into as tiny a ball as I could. With my head down, I could see only his dirty brown boots. They were covered with mud, and I thought he must be one of the men who had chased me through the fens that afternoon.

Simon's feet made a sudden loud clatter on the wooden walkway leading to the drawbridge. Then there was a tinkling noise, as of coins hitting the boards.

"Hell's bells. I opened my purse to give you a farthing and now I've dropped the whole bloody thing."

"What a shame! Let me help you." I could hear the greed through the false sympathy in the man's voice.

"God's teeth, this money has gone everywhere," Simon said.

"Um, mostly farthings, I think." The guard dropped to his knees, facing away from me. Now I could see the soles of his boots, worn and patched under the mud.

"I had some silver though," Simon moaned. "Perhaps it is back here off the path. I think I see a bit of a shine."

The guard moved a few steps further away.

I took a deep breath and started crawling, as quietly and quickly as I could, over the drawbridge. Then I stood up and began to run, throwing caution to the winds, toward the castle.

In the dim light it was gray, not the warm red castle of daylight, but it had never seemed more like home.

I stopped when I saw the figure in the front of the building. Simon had told me there was another guard on duty there.

If I could see him, I knew he could see me. I fell to the ground. Carefully, I began to crawl again, this time away from the entrance and toward the side of the castle. Finally, I reached the side wall and got to my feet. I walked to the back, staying close to the wall. The brick was still faintly warm from the day's sunshine. Out of one of the rear second-story windows of the castle, I could just see a rope hanging. It looked terribly long, and the window seemed far away.

As I stood there looking up, I felt a hand on my shoulder. I jumped, but it was only Simon.

"Well done," he whispered in my ear.

"I don't know if I can do this," I whispered back.

He demonstrated for me, holding the rope in his hands and using his feet against the castle wall for purchase.

I tried then, and fell immediately to the ground. The tug in my arms and elbows was a horror of pain. I had never done anything like this in my life. I wished that I were stronger, or that I had been my brother running around, climbing trees, and rowing boats instead of always being sickly and spending my time reading books in the library. I wished with all my heart that I did not have to do this.

"Remember all you have already done," Simon said, still in a whisper. "Such a strong brave girl I have never seen."

That helped.

"I will boost you up for a start."

He took me by the waist and hoisted me up over his head. I grabbed the rope and began to climb. He then took my feet and supported them till I was past his reach. At that point the pain in my shoulders and arms came back, as before, and I just hung there for a moment. But there was no choice. I had to do this.

I thought of my warm bed at the top. It was not enough. I thought of what I had done, hiding in the swamp, sneaking past the sentry, binding John's wound. It was not enough. Then I thought of the dogs. I imagined that the hounds were below me, barking and snapping, as they had swum behind us on the creek. I began to move. I pulled the hellish rope and placed my feet onto the bricks, and finally there was a sort of rhythm to my motion.

I struggled upwards. I trembled with the effort. My hands were rubbed raw and bleeding by the rope. Finally I saw the sill of the window above me. Now I had a new problem. Somehow I had to pull myself up over the sill. There was no one to help me, though Simon had said he would go back into the castle and try to get to the room to help me. I knew it would take him some time to go around the building and enter, especially since he could not appear to be in a hurry, going past the guard. Then he would have to climb the stairs and get into the room.

I hung there for a moment, and then pulled myself till I could get the window casement in my hand. I was frightened to let go of the rope but I did it. Once I let go I would not be able to crawl back down.

Dogs. Dogs, I told myself as I gritted my teeth and pulled up hard.

I could not do it. I could not lift myself the extra two feet. I simply could not. Without the rope I could not use my feet on the wall for leverage, and I had to somehow pull my entire weight up over the sill. I made one more effort, taking a deep breath, scrambling with my knees against the brick, trying to use them as I had used my feet, and then pushing up with all my strength. I fell back, dangling there, feeling the wrenching pull on my shoulders again. I would not be able to hang there long. I felt like I was being tortured on the rack, my arms pulled out of their sockets. I thought of all I had been through, and then to die, smashed against the ground.

And then there was Simon's dear face, gasping for breath, and his hands pulling me through.

ONCE AGAIN I burst into tears in Simon's arms. This time I was really safe. It took several minutes for me to catch my breath and clear my head. The window I had climbed through was in Simon's bedroom. I could not stay there for more than a few minutes, in case someone came.

"I will sleep with Marianne," I said. I had already thought this through at Davey's. "If I go to my room, the Sheriff's men may notice me. They will not notice one more servant, and I am dressed as a servant."

"I thought you would go back to your room. Patience is frantic. She has been at the chapel praying for two days now. She will be wide awake, waiting for you."

"You go, please, to tell her and my parents that I am safe. You can walk through the castle, but I must be more careful."

Simon surveyed me, squinting in the dark room. "Yes, your insect bites will give you away."

I had given no thought to what my face looked like. There was, of course, no mirror at Davey's. I looked down at my arms, and even in the dark I could see they were mottled with bites upon bites and angry scratch marks. My hands were bleeding from the rope. My face must have looked like my arms.

"I must make my way to Marianne."

I was so tired I could barely stand. I hugged him again. We had never touched before today, but I felt so close to him for helping me. He seemed surprised when I flung my arms around him, but his arms, after an instant, pulled back. I was aware of him as a man, a strong and handsome man whom I cared deeply about. Even better, in my ragged clothes, in terrible need of a bath, covered with insect bites, my hair full of river silt, I knew in my bones that he was aware of me as a woman.

I pulled away, suddenly shy, and began to leave the room.

Simon insisted on checking that there was no one around,

and in a moment I was climbing the stairs in the dark, as I had become used to doing, this time to the fourth floor. I made my way into Marianne's room. Most servants slept in the basement in the servants' quarters, but Marianne, as personal maid to Arbella, had a small room next to her, should she want Marianne in the night.

I stumbled over Marianne's shoes. The noise and my curse wakened her, and she made a small sound as she turned over and opened her eyes. Before she could scream, I spoke. "It is just me. Anne."

She sat up. "Anne, Anne, we thought you were gone for good. Come into bed and tell me."

"I am too tired. In the morning."

I could scarcely take off my shoes, or rather Joan's shoes, and her skirt, before falling into the bed. I had slept at Davey's and thought myself restored, but now I was done. I was asleep in an instant.

# Chapter Eighteen

I HEARD UNFAMILIAR voices. They sounded far away. I opened my eyes and saw two Sheriff's men, one the sentry at the moat, and one whom I had not seen before. I shut my eyes again. It was too hard to keep them open.

"Look how red her face is, and the sores on it. It is the pox, like the Earl's brother. And there was the kitchen maid."

"And the wife of the baker, someone said," another voice added.

"It is time to be gone. A criminal is one matter, but no need for us all to risk death from the pox." The voice had authority.

There was silence again, and I slept.

I was too sick to react to the words. Everything hurt. My head felt like it would explode, waves of nausea passed through me, chills and fever shook me.

There were other words. I knew Patience was there, and took my hand, and Mother admonished her to keep away.

There were hands that lifted me and took me to another place. My head banged against the wall once. When I was laid down, the room felt like Hades.

"Too hot," I pleaded.

"The doctor said heat. He will not come, himself, may the pox take him." It was Mother's voice again.

An uncontrollable spell of shivering hit me, and the heat felt good. Later, in a moment of awareness, I realized I was in my parents' room, on their bed, that I was wrapped in blankets, and that the fire was lit in the fireplace.

I LAY THERE for several days, going from sleep to wakefulness, hot and cold, tossing and turning, in pain from backaches and headaches, not able to find a comfortable way to lie. My dreams were vivid.

I dreamed of John. We were sitting on the river bank, the beggar nearby, and John saying sweet things to me.

This time I said, "If you loved me true, you would not leave me here."

I dreamed it several times in different ways. Once I woke, while saying, "You do not love me true."

John's expression seemed bewildered, until his face gradually dissolved and became that of Marianne.

She took me in her arms, saying, "Many love you."

She understood that I was not speaking of the love of my family, that I was speaking to a man, but she did not pry. She laid me back in the bed, and since I was in a fever state, took off some of the blankets and put a wet cloth on my head.

After a few days, my fever subsided and I felt better. I asked Marianne whether the Earl's sister did not need her.

"You are much too fine a person to spend your time caring for me," I said. "You should be surrounded by taffeta and silk, helping to decide if Arbella should wear mauve or lavender."

She laughed. "Your mother would not hear my protests even if I had any. She scoured the castle, looking for anyone who had suffered the pox and would not fall victim again. There were only me and one of the scullery maids. I do not mind a change from finery."

I told her she was a fine nurse and inwardly prayed that, like Marianne's, my face would not be pocked.

Mother came to see me. I had always known my mother loved me but I had never felt it so keenly. She was risking her life to be with me.

"It is so good…" she began, and then could say no more for the tears.

HER GLADNESS CAME too soon. That night, the rash erupted, all over my body and face. I could feel the little swellings with my finger tips. The fever came back, and I fell into a sleep from which I awoke only once or twice to feel my heart beating uncontrollably, a terrible pain in my chest.

People measured sleep in time: how long did you sleep? And in depth: how deep was it, how hard to wake? This sleep was long and deep, but it seemed to me mostly a broad, wide sleep. It touched parts of me that had never slept before. Blackness engulfed my hands, my feet, my knees, my elbows. I had no thoughts. My mind slept. I did not dream. My heart slept. I did not even pray to God to save me. My soul slept.

Later, I learned what happened while I slept. The red sores became pimples, the pimples became pustules, and they dried into crusts. My skin, hot to the touch, peeled off in limp sheets.

They told me I dwelled in this black place between life and death for a week. Then one day I woke again with pain in my chest, to see Marianne leaning over me.

"Thank the Lord."

I went back to sleep, then woke once again without the chest pain.

"Water."

She brought me some and fed it to me with a spoon.

I slept again, and woke for longer. I drank more.

The next time I woke, Mother was there. She put her arms about me and wept.

"We thought we would lose you," she said, through sobs.

I was too weak to realize, at the time, that I was better, or what she meant. I returned to sleep.

IN THE NEXT few days I began to recover. I remember the day I heard the raspy cries of magpies outside my window and found them beautiful. They had been there every morning, but that was the first time I noticed them. I knew, at that moment, that I would live.

I asked for the window to be uncovered. I began to pay attention to the pattern the sun made as it crossed the room through my sleeping and waking. It was sharp in the morning, in my eyes, and then warm upon my legs, and then there were shadows, and late in the day it was sharp against the other wall.

Marianne was a wonderful nurse. When I woke, she talked to me about what she was doing,

"Now I will put a cool cloth on your brow," or "Eat some fine stewed peaches." I was too tired to speak. Often I went to sleep to the sound of "Tomorrow the Fox will Come to Town," sung in Marianne's sweet, low voice. And woke to the sound of, "Of all the Birds that ever I See," which included words about drinking that Mother would not have approved of.

Mainly, I slept. Gradually my thinking returned, and I began to wonder what had happened while I slept. The next time Mother came into the room, I asked her.

"Everything is fine." She smiled, smoothed my hair, and told me not to worry.

"Has the Earl returned?"

"No. We hear from him regularly. He is in good health and he has not been tortured. There are a number of nobles being held and not brought to trial. Your father is preparing a petition about how prisoners cannot be held without trial; you know, the *habeas corpus* idea he always talks about."

"And John Holland?" I tried to sound like I did not care.

"Thank the Lord, he has escaped to Holland."

My eyes shut, and I felt relief pour through me.

"He may be able to come back at some point. So painful for his wife, and she with child."

"What?" My voice sounded weak and strange.

"You did not know she was with child? She is a fine, healthy lass, and to be without her husband is difficult. At least there has been no warrant out for her."

As she bustled about the room straightening things, Mother went on about John's wife, who she was and her people, but I did not hear her. I was in torment. How could he? I had known he had not truly cared for me or he would not have left me at the river. But how could he have lied to me?

"I see I am tiring you. You are so pale." Mother took up her basin and left the room.

Then the tears came, till I was so weak I fell asleep.


WHEN I WOKE again, not sure whether it was the same day or not, I was calmer. I tried to remember exactly what John had said, when I asked him if he was married. He had not said, "No, I am not married." He had said something like, "I am a good Puritan, and such do not trifle with young women when they are married."

So he was not a good Puritan. I had risked my life to save the life of a man who was willing to ruin me. Had he thought I was simply a loose young woman, willing to walk about the castle at night in her shift? What of the Earl's hospitality? John's duty to my father? Surely he would have known that I would, at some time, learn about his wife.

Lying in bed, I had nothing else to do but think about it. I decided he was the kind of man who did what he felt like doing without thinking of the consequences. I remembered my father had called him hotheaded and impulsive. He had posted all those notices about not paying the tax. I remembered how he had ignored my counsel and chosen his own way in the fens. When I had been there alone with him in the secret room he fancied me, and he did not worry about what would happen later.

I still felt tears welling, but then anger rose within me. I wished I had pushed him into the river. I wanted to get up and find him and do something to him. I did not know what. I began to rise from the bed, fell back, and sank into sleep again.

THE NEXT DAY I needed to distract myself. I was irritable and bored with being in bed, but too sick to get up. I decided to make something of the one good thing that John had given me. I would finish his verse to me.

> *Shall I compare thee to a summer day?*
> *Thou art more lovely and more temperate.*

They were easy end rhymes. One could say,

> *Thy sunny face makes all who see thee gay,*
> *Thy body warm to me as heaven's gate.*

It was not good, but it was fun to play. It made me smile to think of nice things somebody could say of me. I forgot about the sin of Vanity. I had come up with several other rhymes when I heard footsteps in the hallway. Patience came through my door and jumped onto the bed to embrace me through the blankets and coverlet.

"I have missed you so!" I hugged her back.

We talked of what I had done, and I told her what Mother had said about John's wife. Her loving nature took in all my badness and turned it into good. She saw only my attempt to help John and the family, not my wantonness or desire for adventure. I told her all, as Marianne says Catholics tell their confessor, and I could see why Catholics value this cleansing.

Finally, I said, "Patience, there is something only you will do for me. Please, I want the mirror."

Marianne and Mother had refused. They claimed my face was not bad, but why, then, would they not bring the mirror? Marianne had no marks at all from the pox, but I was sure I would have them. They had forbidden me to touch my face. Of course as soon as I was alone I did, and I could feel sores with my fingers.

"No, you should wait a bit till it has time to heal."

"Then it is bad."

"No, not so bad."

"Then bring the mirror."

After a while she brought it, Mother's precious mirror of Venetian glass trimmed in gold, three inches across. I took a deep breath and held it up before my face.

There were fifteen to twenty bright, red spots. They were not so different from mosquito bites, and I could see how the Sheriff's men had earlier been misled. That thought came later, though. I put the mirror face down on the coverlet and tried not to weep. The tears came anyway.

"They will heal and fade," Patience said, in her sweet, determined voice. She distracted me with tales about the little things that had happened in the castle, how one of the servants had taken a bad fall down the stairs, breaking his leg, and how I should look forward to a visit from Mercy.

Then my father came. I had been dreading this visit.

"You are better, I see. You've worried us terribly."

"I'm sorry."

"What kind of girl did I raise, to traipse around the country with a married man? Have you learned nothing from your mother about what is proper? I give you the best education any girl or boy could desire, and you reward me by acting like a common…"

He couldn't find a word that was decent enough to speak to his daughter. His voice was the loudest thing I had heard in the sick room, and perhaps he could tell it wearied me.

"I did save his life." My voice sounded feeble to my own ears.

"Much better for him to save his own life."

I did not know what he meant, or if he was clear himself about what he meant. "It was the story about the walnuts and the battle of Amiens that helped Simon and me get me back in the castle."

Then Father told the story again, his anger abating as he told it. I was so relieved his voice was softer that I listened as though I had never heard the tale before. I asked him several times what would happen to our family, and he would not tell me.

THE NEXT DAY Patience brought a book. It was a slim one I had not seen before.

"I found it with the forbidden books," she said with a blush. She explained that after the Sheriff's men knocked down the door to the secret room, they went through the books. None were traitorous. They were the kind of work that the King, and Protestants, and Catholics also, liked, which was why the Earl had locked them up as not suited for Puritans. So the men left them, with some broken bindings and torn pages. Father decided simply to put them on the library shelf, trusting to our judgment as to whether to read them. Patience had gone through them and found this one she thought I would like. It was titled *Shakespeare's Sonnets*.

She put it on the bed, and I held it up. I had never read his poetry. It would be a lovely book to read while I was recovering.

"And look what I have found in the middle," she said, in a tone of wonderment.

She held out a thin paper, yellowing, with faint-brown ink. It was a family tree for the Dudley family. It was hard to make out, especially since my mind was not working at its best yet. Perhaps it would say who Father's grandfather was, whom he always spoke of proudly but with a mysterious air. He would never tell us his name. I found Father's father, Roger Dudley. There was Roger's father, someone named George Dudley.

"George is the man that Father talks of who led such an adventurous life, having to leave the country, and fighting the Saracen when he was fifteen." My voice grew brighter as I remembered the stories.

"Yes, and he is our great-grandfather."

"So why did Father not say so? He is always hinting at our noble ancestors, and saying we could use a coat of arms if we chose, but he never answers when I ask him."

I put the paper down, and was running the edges of the coverlet through my fingers as I tried to figure it out.

Patience had thought about it longer. "He was involved in uprisings against the King, maybe more than one King, and it would be dangerous to let people know that you were descended from such a man."

She was probably right. After she left, I thought more about it. It was good to be of noble blood, but when you could not tell anyone, did it matter?

I wondered what George was like when he was my age. Would I have liked him? What could we have talked about? His life was so wild, escaping from prison and becoming a knight at fifteen. Mine was so ordinary. Then I remembered how I had bound up John's wounds and landed the boat. I smiled and fell back to sleep, the Shakespeare carefully hidden under the coverlets.

## CHAPTER NINETEEN

THE NEXT DAY the sun woke me, and I pulled out my book. When I heard steps on the stone outside, I thrust Shakespeare back under the blanket. It was only Marianne, who did not care about books that might contain wicked thoughts. She carried my porridge on a large trencher that I could balance on my lap.

I spooned it slowly, as I still had little appetite, and it was cold. Mother was right about how long it took to carry the food upstairs.

We talked about the day, the sunny weather I was missing while lying about. I had been sick for weeks. The summer was coming to an end.

"When are you going to introduce me to Simon?" she asked, with no preamble.

"Soon, when I am up and about."

It sounded vague to my own ears. I knew I no longer wanted to. My feelings had changed. I began to tell Marianne about our ancestor and some of Father's stories about him.

After she left I napped, then took out my book. I found a line Shakespeare had stolen from my favorite poet, Bartas, about all the world being a stage. Then I turned some pages and beheld:

*Shall I compare thee to a Summer's day?*
*Thou art more lovely and more temperate.*

Such a pain in my heart. I knew that John had not really cared for me, but this poem had been a kind of gift, one of the few loving things that he had said. But he was untrue even in this. My face grew hot as the tears flowed. My chest heaved, but I did not cry out. I did not want Marianne to come. This was my own grief, and no one could share it, not even Patience. I cried and cried.

And then curiosity won out over sorrow. I opened the book again to see the rest of the poem. Shakespeare's rhymes were so much stronger than anything I had been able to create. At least John had recognized a beautiful poem. When I reached the last lines,

*So long as men can breathe, or eyes can see,*
*So long lives this, and this gives life to thee.*

the hair stood up on my arms, and tears came to my eyes again, in a different way. I read the words again and again, to see what made them wrench my insides. They were two lines of the simplest of words, all one syllable, most of them three or four letters. It was not a poem about a pretty woman, it was a poem about how poetry can give life to things that die. I said the words over and I felt comfort.

I knew then that reading poems was not enough. I wanted to write them.

I tried to get up to find a quill and paper. I pushed myself out of bed and onto my feet for the first time, but I was immediately dizzy and fell back onto the blankets. I could not write yet, but I would. I would practice and I would learn.

For the remainder of the day, I made up rhymes in my head. Later, I did manage to push myself out of bed to go to the necessary. My legs shook under me, and I laughed to myself, thinking I could never climb the castle wall now.

But I am getting better, I told myself. As I got back into the bed, I heard unfamiliar steps outside and wondered if they were coming towards me. Everyone had visited me except Simon and Sarah and Baby Mercy. I saw Mother and Patience every day.

It was Mercy, looking different somehow. Taller? Thinner? Had she grown up in the few weeks of my illness? She gave me a hug and kiss.

"Such gladness I feel at your recovery," she said, and even her voice sounded less high-pitched. It was "such," not "thuch" gladness.

"What happened to your lisp?"

She shrugged and ran her hands over her skirt.

"Went away, I guess."

"Has Sarah stopped bothering you?"

She nodded. "Mostly. Next time we go to Boston, will you take me to get a new bonnet? Mother is so old fashioned."

"Yes, we will find something with a frill."

She danced out of the room.

SIMON, LAST OF my visitors, came the next day. His hair was well brushed, and he seemed uncomfortable.

I felt awkward myself. I wondered how ugly my scabs looked. I did not know, as I hadn't looked in the mirror since Patience brought it the first time. I was glad there was not too much light in the room. I made some comment about his empty hands, and how I had expected him to bring me something to study.

He did not respond, and said only, "You're better, I can see."

"I have survived, but I am scarred."

"You have always been a comely lass and you are still."

His eyes were even finer and darker than I remembered. His voice seemed strained. I felt even more uncomfortable, and asked him to sit on the stool beside the bed. The legs were not quite even, and for a moment the only sound was the rocking of the stool as he tried to make it settle.

"I was hoping you would come," I said, and blushed. "I wanted news," I added.

"What would you like to know?"

"Mother said our visitor escaped."

"That beggar in Boston approached me, asking for money. He said he had paid his own money to put John on the boat to Holland."

I made a doubtful noise.

"My thought, also. I asked him why I would give money to a scoundrel who had left my employer's daughter to wander through the fens." He began to imitate the beggar's Scottish tones.

"'Ay, she'll have done fine. A stout-hearted lass. Isn't she fine, then?'"

"I hope you told him I drowned in the swamp."

Simon snorted. I was beginning to feel more comfortable.

"I told him you had the pox. That turned him pale, all right."

I laughed. "So you did not give him any money."

"In the end I gave him a bit. I think John probably had money."

I nodded. "Maybe not quite enough."

There was another silence. Simon had stopped trying to settle the stool.

"You have asked about John and not about what will happen to the family. Do you have tender feelings for him?"

I blushed again and shook my head, and then realized I must account for the blush.

"I did when he came. He was handsome and charming. I was alone with him after never knowing any men."

"You knew me."

I was surprised when he said that. It took me a long time to answer. "You never acted like a man with a woman. I was always a pupil to you. A silly, sentimental pupil," I added bitterly, quoting his words. I looked down and began to run the fringe of the coverlet through my fingers.

"I was angry when I said that. I'm sorry. I always admired your ability, Anne."

This seemed a difficult topic for both of us, and I returned to our original subject.

"Anyway, in the end I saw John as he is, and I do not like or honor him."

Simon nodded. "He should not have left you."

"No."

We were silent again. I was still busy with the coverlet when I asked him what would happen to the family.

"The Sheriff reported everything to the King, of course. The King needs money so badly for his wars that he said he would not prosecute the Earl or your father if they lent him a large sum of money."

"Not so different from lending money to the beggar man," I said.

"Yes. No hope of its return."

"That is what will happen?"

He hesitated. "You know how your father is about money. He actually asked me how much I lost when I spilled my purse at the guard house."

"He repaid you? And for what you gave to Davey?"

He laughed. "Not yet."

I noted that Simon was stealing glances at me, and I wondered what he was thinking of my pockmarks.

"Will he pay the money to the King? He must, I think."

"We shall see. I think he plans to delay for a while."

At that moment Marianne entered the room, color in her cheeks and very pretty. She must have known that Simon was there.

"Is all well?" she asked.

I said yes and found I did not want to introduce her to Simon, she so fresh and blond and I so gaunt and pocked. There were many things I could have said about her, how well she had cared for me, her good humor, her intelligence, but I said only that she was Arbella's private servant.

Simon had risen when she came in. "Good to know your name. I have seen you, of course. I'll come back another time, Anne."

And he was gone, leaving both of us disappointed.

Marianne left as well, but I saw her again when she came back to bring my supper. As she laid the tray upon my lap she did not look me in the eye. She helped me put the napkin on my neck and took the cover off the porridge, all without a word.

"I am sorry," I mumbled, as I took a drink of milk.

"You talk so grandly about tolerance. Simon would not care that I am Catholic. And then you introduce me like that. You have no tolerance yourself, you think because I am a servant I should not have ideas above my station—"

"If I thought you were only a servant I would not allow you to speak so to me."

She paid no attention to my reproving words. However angry she was, she knew we were friends. She looked at me sharply. "I thought you did not fancy him."

"I thought he was handsome but, as I told you, he always seemed to care only about books and ideas. When he rescued me we became closer. But now he again seems to have no feeling for me."

"Ha," was all she said. There was more silence as she waited for me to finish eating. I tried to spoon up the porridge quickly, but I was still not myself, and I had to take small mouthfuls and swallow slowly.

She turned away from me and looked out the window. It was still light, though the day was gray and overcast. She began to hum softly.

An idea flashed through my mind. "Marianne, do you know Davey, the baker?"

"No. Why would Arbella's maid go on errands to the bakery?" She sounded distant.

"Well, you should." I explained who Davey was and how he had helped me, and how handsome he was, and about his wife's death, and how she had hummed.

"Find a reason to go to the bakery. Tell Davey I need one of his rolls for my recovery. And hum."

Marianne had gone back to looking out the window, though she turned to answer me. "Your notions about men are not likely to excite me again. Do I want a baker, so I can live in a hovel?"

"It is not a hovel. It is clean, and warm all winter from the oven, and has pictures on the wall."

I didn't say that there was one old picture of Queen Elizabeth and a small wall hanging of wool.

"And I suppose he told you he is Catholic?"

"No. But he is brave, and if he were a strong Puritan he would not have Queen Elizabeth's picture on the wall. She was tolerant of Catholic and Puritan alike, and he admires her. What other men will you meet here at the castle, especially now that the Earl is gone and there are no visitors?"

"That last part is true. There are no men for me here except laborers covered with mud from the fields, or smelling of eels from the fens, and spending their few farthings at the tavern." She snatched my tray, though I had several mouthfuls of porridge remaining, and took it away as I protested that Davey did not go to the tavern.

# Chapter Twenty

THAT NIGHT I began feeling better and practiced getting up and walking down the castle passageways. I felt so accomplished. I was reminded of when Baby Mercy was an actual baby, beginning to walk. We all clapped, and I wrote down how many steps she had taken each day, until there were too many to count.

Mother observed me staggering along the castle wall and decided it was time to reclaim her room. I was able to walk to my room by myself, though Mother held one elbow and I pressed my other hand to the brick.

It was fun to sleep with Patience again, and we stayed up late talking about what Simon had told me and whether Father would pay the King the money he wanted. In the morning, I tried to get up for breakfast but fell back into the bed. Marianne brought me my porridge and said that Arbella needed her and that she must return to her care. I thanked her. My voice felt strained, and she did not look me in the eye.

THAT NOON I got up, put on a skirt over my shift, straightened my hair and put on a bonnet, and took my place by Sarah at the table.

Everyone was there, including Father, though Simon did not appear. Everyone greeted me gladly, and even Sarah said, "Welcome." I saw her staring at my pockmarks, and when I looked back at her, she flushed and looked away. At least she did not whisper, "How ugly you are!" the way she might have in the past.

Father said the grace. I had been savoring the thought of my first real meal and I took an immediate, large sip of ale. The servants served us the food, then left. The leg of lamb looked heavenly. As I prepared to cut into my slice of meat, my head already buzzing from the ale, Father tapped the table.

"Now that Anne has joined us and we are all here, I have an announcement to make." He was using his important voice.

He began as though he was telling one of his stories, but it was our story, the story of what had happened to our family since Sarah had posted Simon's paper on the board in Boston market. He told about John and about how I had foolishly accompanied him. He knew many details of the trip that Simon must have told him.

"The consequences of all these events are the following: The King has demanded large sums of money from us, Anne's reputation has been damaged, and she may never marry."

Once again I waited for Sarah to whisper, "It is because you are so ugly," but she restrained herself.

"I was planning to send you away," he said, looking at Sarah, "but I have found a better way to punish your wayward soul."

He paused and looked around the table with a satisfied glance.

"We are going to the New World."

It was as though he had said, "We are going to fly to the moon." We hardly reacted because we could not believe it.

Mother finally said, "What nonsense is this?"

I could see how upset she was, calling Father's words nonsense. When he did not reply with anger, I was astonished.

"I am not joking, Dorothy. We are going to New England, in the New World."

"Why, when?" She stammered, not able even to ask what she wanted to know.

"There is no other solution. We can join the other Puritans in that land and worship without fear. This country will soon be broken in two by a religious war, Puritans against Catholics. You do not want your son killed in battle and your daughters slaughtered for their religion.

"Then there is the matter of the money the King is demanding. It will not take long for him to take everything the Earl and I have. We shall call the ship the *Arbella*."

That detail somehow made it real. We were going to get into a ship called the *Arbella* and sail, who knew how many miles, across the ocean.

"It will be good for our souls. We will have to leave most of our things behind. There will be no more fancy hats, or frills on bonnets and petticoats, or silk, or leg of lamb and sugar cakes."

He gestured to our meal, lying cold on our plates, as we gaped at him. "Very little sugar at all." He looked hard at Sarah.

Her lower lip trembled and she jiggled her foot under the table.

"May I be excused?" she said, in a low voice.

"No, I want you to sit here and see the pain you have caused."

Mother's face was drawn and white. I was surprised that Father had not told her earlier.

"My beautiful house in Boston..." was all she said, and then the tears began to stream silently down her cheeks.

"Will Simon come with us?" I asked.

"He will have to decide," Father replied.

I realized later that it was of Simon that I thought, not John, though I knew John was going to the New World.

Sarah could no longer hold her tears, and they burst out. She rose and went to the other side of the table, where she threw her arms around Mother's neck.

"I'm sorry," she sobbed.

Mother, stiff at first, melted and put her arms around Sarah.

"Enough," she said to Father. "She is only a child. You may all leave the table."

And we did, although we had barely touched the meal. Mother had her way over Father in one small respect.


I WENT BACK to bed while the others resumed their day's activities. I thought all day and could barely wait till Patience came to bed. Would we survive? Would we be killed by Indians or by wild beasts? Would there be servants or could we manage without them? Would I have any time to write? How would my health be in a different climate? I had heard the winters of New England were fiercely cold, while the summers were much hotter than here in England.

When Patience came to bed, we talked mainly of what could we bring. It was less frightening than these other questions.

How many bonnets? Could we bring stiff ones that needed to sit on a frame? Would we need warmer clothes? Or more clothes for warm weather?

I had ruined my best dress and then burned it in Davey's oven. I could smell the burning silk in my mind, yet. Would I ever get another best dress? Father had said no silk. Would we bring only practical clothes, bonnets to cover the head rather than to look fetching, boots rather than shoes, colors that didn't show the dirt?

"Father will probably let us bring our chest with our clothes in it." Patience was optimistic, as always.

We looked over at the chest. We knew it to be completely full, and many of our things did not fit into it. Shoes and boots lined up along the wall, and bonnets stood in boxes.

"We will need new things. At least we can shop. I saw the most beautiful green wool bonnet in Boston last winter," Patience said. "Or we could see what New England is like and buy things there. Oh."

There was silence as we both realized that we could buy nothing there, that there was no merchandise that did not come from England. We would have to bring everything we would ever need, unless goods came later on a ship from England.

We stopped talking then, but it was a long time before either of us fell asleep.

# Chapter Twenty-One

WEEKS PASSED. I regained my strength quickly, now, and went back to life as it had been. Some things changed, however.

Father insisted that we do more of the servants' work, so that when we got to the New World we would know how to care for ourselves.

"Think like a peasant! Look about you in the village! Soon you will be living in a hut with animals and vermin, and the smell of the hearth always about you and your clothes."

Father seemed to delight in the prospect. I was not sure whether he thought of it as mortification, like Catholic saints do for their souls, or whether he saw it as an adventure. A little of both, I thought.

We would take some servants, but nothing like what we had at the castle. I spent hours with Cook, learning the herbs of the garden and the castle village. We seldom ate greens, but we would rely on them in a new country. Most I already knew, but there were a few—borage and orach and southernwood and salad burnet—that I confused with other plants. I learned which mushrooms could be safely eaten.

I wondered if the plants would be the same, or whether I would have to learn new ones, and who would teach me. Would there be magpies and sparrows, damselflies, and ducks?

I learned to make pies, and bake bread, and create stews of all varieties, and how to put a bird upon a spit in the oven, and how to prepare eel pies. Would there be eels in the New World? Here there was little else but eels.

The greater change in me was one that nobody else saw, even Patience. I began to make up verses, but only in my head, not on the page. While I picked borage and rosemary, I rhymed them with storage and carry. I made up poems about the castle and the fens. I made a silly poem about eel pie. I started to make up a sad poem about John, but I did not like it, and did not finish it. I made up poems about the family, many about Sarah, who was quieter than she had been. Still, there were times when I saw flashes of the old spirit in her eyes.

I made up poems about Simon. Father had stopped my lessons. There would be no books to read in the New World unless we brought them.

I saw Simon, occasionally, when he came with Father to our meals. He seemed distant, though he was always kind when he spoke to me. I wondered if he was seeing Marianne. I saw her seldom and I missed her. I missed Simon more; his company, his wit, his thick dark hair, his large dark eyes, his mouth.


I FOUND MYSELF waiting, each day, to see if Simon would come to dinner. Finally, one day at dinner, when he had not arrived, Father announced that Simon was moving away from us, to Boston. I almost cried out, I felt the pain so strongly.

As soon as the meal was over I ran to the roof. There was a fine mist in the air, and I could not tell how much of the wet on my cheeks was tears and how much was rain.

What did I feel about Simon? I had first loved him as a kind of father. Better than my own father as a teacher, Simon was patient and gentle. I had loved him as an older brother. I had grown up with him. Now I wanted to love him as a man, and he was gone.

I was deep in these thoughts, looking out at the fens without seeing them, when I heard steps behind me. I turned, and there was Simon.

"It was there that I found you coming back from the fens," he said, pointing to the tree-lined path, leading away.

"It was I who found you, is how I think of it." I might be losing him, but I could not be spiritless. "What are you doing up on the roof?" I asked him. "You have never come before."

"I have often seen you heading up the stairs and I knew you were not going to the fourth floor to visit the Earl."

I felt easier. He had come looking for me. Whatever happened, he still held me in regard.

We said nothing for a while. We were both leaning over the railing toward the south, not looking at each other. I glanced toward him and saw beads of moisture begin to collect along his hairline, from the mist.

"Father said you were leaving us."

He sighed. "I cannot stay here any longer."

My heart grew sore again.

"It's because of you. I don't want to treat you as John did," he went on.

I didn't know what he meant, and turned to look at him. He looked at me also, and he must have seen my puzzled expression.

"Taking advantage of your being a child—"

"I am not a child," I interrupted indignantly. We were now facing each other and our voices were loud.

"Fifteen is still a child."

"I will be sixteen in the spring."

"I was your tutor, supposed to be teaching you, not drawn to you."

"Aha. So you did feel something."

"Yes, but I would never take advantage."

"No, you never did. But you could have been a little more human, a little less like a stick—"

"No. I couldn't. All my feelings might have come out."

"And these last months, is that why you have abandoned me, never helping me through what has been a difficult time for me, because your feelings might have come out?"

"Yes, I didn't want to take advantage of that hellish experience we went through together. I feared that you would believe you owed me something—"

"Because you helped to save my life," I interrupted again.

"You saved your own life. You are the bravest woman I have ever met."

Tears sprang to my eyes, and I looked away. He had called me a brave girl before, but this was the first time he had called me a woman.

"And now, when you have been sick, I would be taking advantage of that as well."

"How are you taking advantage? What you mean is that I am ugly now, with pockmarks on my face."

"Have you ever thought that, for some men, beauty is not the only attribute they want in a woman? That intelligence, and strength, and kindness are more important?"

"So you do think I'm ugly. Smart and strong and kind and ugly. You don't want me. You probably want Marianne." Yelling at him made me feel better.

"Ha! I don't want you, do I? What do you think I dream of at night? Nothing but a girl who smells like mud and sweat, and has ripped clothes, and beautiful eyes that are full of light."

133

He pulled me to him and began to kiss me, hard, on the lips. It was nothing like being kissed by John, which was sweet and dreamy. This was like life itself.

With no words at all, we knew we would be together.

We stayed a long time. It began to rain harder, but we did not notice. Finally, Simon broke away, and we looked at each other—our hair plastered to our heads, our clothes soaked through. I was sure that, for the rest of my life, the taste of rain water would make my knees weak.

Simon hugged me again and as he helped me down the stairs, he said only, "I will talk to your father."

That night, as I fell asleep, I had the first line of a poem in my head.

*If ever two were one, then surely we.*

## Chapter Twenty-Two

Simon and I married when I was sixteen, in a small celebration. I had a fine new dress of blue silk, one I probably would have few chances to wear again but that I could bring to the New World. We enjoyed sweetmeats and fine wine and a lovely cake.

That night, after the others had left, Simon took me in his arms. "I wonder," he said, "if we would have found each other without that one summer's day you journeyed through the fens."

"It was only one day? It felt like weeks."

"Afternoon of one day to night of the next, just a little more than twenty-four hours."

"I only know we have found each other now."

A few months after Simon and I were betrothed, I passed Marianne, glowing, on the stairs. She smiled as she said hello. When I went to bed that night I found, sitting on a plate on my trunk, a roll with sugar icing in the form of a cross upon it. I knew the significance of the cross. Years before, Queen Elizabeth had forbidden rolls with a Catholic cross on them, except at Easter, and it was not Easter. Marianne had confessed her religion to Davey, and he had accepted her in spite of it. The roll was a thank you from Davey to me.

The Earl had been allowed to return to the castle after ten months in the Tower. He seemed a little paler and thinner, but not otherwise changed. He, also, planned to come to the New World, though not on our voyage. When I asked Simon why the King was letting us go, he said that the King encouraged settlements in the New World as a way of getting rid of troublemakers, while whatever money the settlers made from exports, like lumber and crops, was subject to English taxes.

*Southhampton, England — Easter Sunday, March 27, 1630*

IT TOOK OVER two years of preparation. Finally, the *Arbella* and three smaller sister ships were ready to push off to sea. At the end there were sad farewells with the Earl's family, and most of our servants, and Marianne and Davey. I gave Marianne a small tapestry from my room for her new home, as well as the clothes I could not bring with me.

We set sail with a man named Winthrop, appointed to be our governor. I thought Father should be governor. I thought it was Father's temper that swayed people to appoint Master Winthrop.

No sooner had our four small ships left port than we were buffeted by a storm so terrible that even the captain and sailors were frightened. The swearing was far worse than anything Father had ever uttered. People spewed all about, and the stench down in the hold was unspeakable. I never got seasick, even in the storm, but the smell in the hold was so bad that I vomited.

When we could kneel without being flung about, we prayed mightily. We fasted. No one really wanted to eat, anyway, so it was not much sacrifice to God.

The storm lasted three days and then gradually abated. We had been traveling south along the English coast, but had made little headway. We went ashore for a bit to recover, and so the sailors could clean the boat.

Yellow daffodils covered an English hill. I felt tears in my eyes. Knowing I might never see them again, I dug up a bulb and put it in my pocket, hoping I could plant it in the New World.

THE NEXT DAY we left England behind forever. Patience and I stood at the rail and watched our country disappear, fainter and fainter, until we could no longer tell whether the line at the horizon was land or mist.

We had not gone far when, in the distance, one of the sailors spied eight dots on the horizon.

As we watched, they gradually took on the shape of ships. Everyone crowded on deck. Patience pulled my arm and said, "Perhaps they will come aboard and the men will tell us what we will find in the New World."

Then I heard the captain say to Father, who was standing by him, "They fly no flag."

One of the sailors nearby shouted, "God's eyes! Pirates!"

The captain hushed him, but everyone had heard. Patience grabbed my hand tightly. The captain ordered more and more sail, the ship groaned, and we slipped along faster than we had ever gone, even in the storm.

We stayed on the deck and watched, hoping to see the ships fall back, but instead they grew in size.

The captain kept his watch by the rail, peering through his glass. When he put it down his face was grave. After a deliberation with Master Winthrop, Father, and Simon, he turned to everyone and spoke.

"We shall fight!"

The sailors raised huzzahs, and a hushed murmur went through the passengers. Father's face was flushed, and he shook his fist. Master Winthrop looked pale but determined.

"Fire is the danger," the Captain continued. "Tear down these cabins on the deck, then throw overboard everything that can burn, the bedding especially."

Simon came to me and put his arm about me, whispering reassuring words, and calling me his brave woman, as he often does. Simon said that the ship could withstand a good deal of buffeting and cannon holes and broken masts without sinking, but that if it caught fire it would sink, and we would all be drowned.

In a few minutes the sailors destroyed the little cabins that some of the poorer Puritans had built so carefully on the deck.

We women raced below decks, hauling up blankets and pillows and coverlets and tossing them over the rails. The sea looked like the washing-up water, full of bits and pieces of things that could no longer be identified.

Mother came running up, her arms full of our blue feather comforter. Patience and I watched it float away, and Patience said, "If we survive the pirates, we shall die from the cold."

The captain had signaled the other ships in our little fleet, the sailors had pulled down most of the sail, and the ship turned to face the enemy. And then there was a cry from the sailor poised on the mast.

"Flag, flag ahoy."

We saw that the lead ship hurrying towards us had hoisted the English colors.

We all fell to our knees, as though we were one person. "Hosannah," rang over the water. The sailors joined our noise, but their cries were more rude.

The ships came alongside, and men came aboard. It was fine to see other Englishmen, to know we were not alone on the broad water.

The next morning, as we went to sleep, we missed our comforter. Mother said she hoped it was not so cold as some said, in the new land. That day we fell asleep like babies.

WE SLEPT IN shifts because there was not enough room in the tiny boat for everyone to sleep at night. Most of the three hundred passengers slept in the hold, crowded together like eels in a bucket. We women from the wealthier families had a room to ourselves. It was only enough to hold one bed and two cots, with no place to step around them.

Patience, Mercy, Sarah, I, and Mother slept in the morning, from six o'clock until two in the afternoon. It was often hard to go below to sleep then, with the light strong, though of course once we got to our room below deck it was always dark. John Winthrop's wife and her girls slept in the afternoon. Lady Arbella had the right to sleep at night with her husband. I worried about Lady Arbella, as she was pale and sickly. None of us were used to the hard life; the cold, the dampness, the lack of good food and privacy, but she least of all, and she seemed the most affected.

Simon slept at night, with the large group in the hold. I missed his company, as he was always involved with Father and Master Winthrop.

The rocking of the boat was sometimes pleasant to fall asleep to and sometimes not. When I could not drop off, images flashed through my mind of waves crashing over the boat, sinking us, drowning us in our beds. None of us could swim, of course. I sometimes thought of my other boat trip, and wondered whether life would be a continual adventure, and whether I wanted that.

After a week, we settled into monotony, nothing to see but our ship, the rocking up and down, the spray wetting everything. The odor of the sea was gone, and one of the sailors told Simon that what we think is the smell of the sea is really the smell of the place where the sea meets the land. I wanted that smell again. Instead there was only the stench of all of us crowded into this tiny boat; us and the animals. Most of the animals went into the other boats, but we had a few cows and chickens below decks to provide milk and eggs. The chickens merely clucked, but the cows bellowed to be milked, and bellowed to be fed, and perhaps bellowed because they were frightened. Children cried, sometimes for hours, hungry, cold children who could not be comforted.

The birds were gone, the gulls and the others that had hovered around us at the start. There was nothing to see but occasional fish. Some were strange, different from anything I have seen, with wings above the water. Some were huge, and some chased each other around and seemed to play. Sometimes one of the men caught one—a porpoise it was called—and we ate it. Once we saw a whale that spouted and played and threatened to sink the boat. Finally it left us.

Meals were plain. Generally we ate oatmeal or hard biscuits and cheese, with ale or cider. At the beginning we had a bit of smoked meat, until we ran out, and what was left turned rancid. The smoked fish lasted, and sometimes there was fresh fish. There were no vegetables after the first days, except dried beans and onions, and even the onions began to rot after a time in the damp hold. Vegetables were not my favorite food, but I missed them. The chickens stopped laying and the cows stopped giving milk. What there was went to the young children. The cider tasted good to me, and I drank more than my share. Almost everything was eaten cold because of the risk of fire on board.

Often I would find Sarah on the deck reading her Bible. The first time, I was astounded, but it became commonplace. She turned not only holy, but acted as though she knew more about religion than any of us. She spoke teachings like a minister and she chided us for all our missteps. Once I told her that to be truly Christian was to be charitable. She just made a face at me, not that different from the faces she made when she was seven.

We traveled day after day, till it seemed that the sea must be endless and we would go on forever. Everything became wet, and I was often colder than I had ever been in my life, except for the time I was so drenched in the fens and had to walk back to the castle. I would hear Mother muttering that she wished she could have her drafty castle back again.

ONE DAY THE captain began to take soundings, and though he found no bottom, we knew the end of our journey was near. I saw the first gull, and after a day or two we smelled land again. On June sixth, we saw land for the first time. We traveled south for a few days till we found the harbor we sought.

We could see the settlement, just a few huts, cruder than anything that the poorest villagers lived in at the castle. Davey's house was grand in comparison. None of these roofs had the neat thatching I was used to. I guessed that there were none of the reeds we had in such abundance in the English fens. Simon said someone had brought reeds along so that we could plant them.

There were a few wisps of smoke curling from a chimney or two, and a slight smell of smoke, though mainly the smell of mud. We had come far from the fens, only to return to their smell. And surrounding this small patch of mud there was only forest. Trees, trees, everywhere. We were exchanging one sea for another. There were no clearings, no light in the forest. As far as the eye could see. Full of Indians, wolves, and bears.

At the thought of what lay ahead for us, for Simon and me, for my family—what difficulties, what want of the basic necessities of life, like food and shelter and warmth—my stomach began to churn. Then I remembered that it was Arbella, not I, who was sick

141

from the trip. And I remembered how I had submerged myself in mud when the Sheriff's men were looking for me, and how I had climbed the castle wall.

My stomach calmed as I prepared to disembark with the others. The bravest woman Simon knew was quite able to deal with danger and privation.

# AFTERWORD

ANNE IS MY ancestor, and I thank my mother for some of the research into her life. This is a work of historical fiction. The essentials are true, but I have made up conversations and some incidents like Anne's travel through the fens. I have tried to portray behavior that is consistent with the way she describes herself at fourteen.

## WHAT HAPPENED TO THEM

*Anne Dudley Bradstreet* is recognized as the first woman poet in America. That first year in Massachusetts, none of the Puritans could have imagined such an outcome. Arbella, her husband, and others died of the hardships. Many of the settlers returned to England. Gradually, however, a new Boston was established.

*Anne and Simon* began a family and eventually had eight children, four girls and four boys. Anne managed to develop her skill as a poet while bringing up the children in the wilderness. She wrote of the happiness of her marriage, how much she missed Simon when he was away, and of the children. She was one of the first women to write so intimately about her life. She also wrote poems about historical events and women in history. Simon probably enjoyed these, but the language of almost four hundred years ago makes the poems difficult for today's reader. In this story I haven't used the archaic language of that time, but kept some of its formality.

*John Winthrop* was discovered in dishonest behavior and was forced to resign as governor. Winthrop had been appointed, not elected, and now an election was held.

*Anne's father* became the first elected governor of the Massachusetts Bay Colony.

Later, *Simon* was also elected governor of Massachusetts, served twice, and played a major role in the development of the colony. Some said that if he had still been governor, the witch trials in Salem would never have happened. You can read about this time in *The Book of Maggie Bradstreet*, a novel I wrote about Anne's granddaughter at the time of the witch trials.

*Anne and her sister Mercy* became close later in life, as their husbands were friends, and the two families settled the town of Andover together. It was Mercy's husband who took Anne's poems to England to get them published.

*Sarah* remained a rebel. She began preaching, and she might have been thrown out of the colony if her husband hadn't taken her back to England. He wrote back to her father, claiming that Sarah was adulterous and had given him a disease.

Sarah came home to Boston in the Colonies, and with a great deal of difficulty, her father arranged a divorce for her. Puritans were opposed to divorce under almost any circumstances. Sarah began having relationships with men and started preaching on street corners again. Her father found another husband for her, but Sarah was excommunicated from the church for "odious, lewd, and scandalous, unclean behavior."

She died at thirty-nine, poor and alone. Was she really so wicked? What might have happened to her in a more religiously tolerant environment, or one which allowed women more freedom?

*Anne's* health was never good, but she survived many illnesses. She died at fifty-nine, of a chronic disease that caused her to become thin and weak. It might have been tuberculosis, or perhaps cancer, we don't know. Simon lived many years afterwards.


## The Characters and Their Lives

Most of what we know about Anne Dudley Bradstreet comes from her poems and writings, and she wrote only briefly, in a notebook scribbled over by a child, about her early life. She said that by age six or seven she was reading the Bible and trying to be good. She was sickly as a girl, perhaps with malaria from the fens, which was common from the fifteenth century on in that part of England. Others have suggested a rheumatic heart.

At fourteen, she became aware of her "carnal" feelings, allowed the "follies of youth" to take hold of her, and felt "loose from God." She developed smallpox shortly after this time. Three years later she was married to Simon Bradstreet and was traveling to the New World on the *Arbella*. She wrote that when she saw the coast of New England her stomach rose within her.

John Winthrop writes in his diary that Anne's father was hot-headed and stingy, characteristics that led the Massachusetts Bay Colony investors to reject him, initially, as governor and to appoint Winthrop instead.

Her father did brag about noble ancestors, and one biographer speculates that the ancestor was George Dudley, the adventurer who was a spy at age fifteen and became one of the Knights of Malta. Anne's poem about her father shows real affection and a close relationship with him, in spite of his character flaws. She writes about her mother in a more distant manner, describing her as a good Puritan and a good manager of the household.

We know the details about the trip to America on the *Arbella* from John Winthrop's diary. There was a storm, and the Puritans did throw all the bedding overboard when they feared pirates.

Smallpox was a plague at that time, and there was no real treatment or understanding of how it spread. Heat was prescribed by some doctors. We don't know if Anne was left with pockmarks. Smallpox takes some time to incubate, so she would not have caught it from Davey's wife's clothes, but probably from the market in Boston or from somebody in the castle.

## HISTORY OF THE TIMES

In 1623, the English heir to the throne, Charles, had indeed crossed Europe in disguise to woo a Spanish princess, who refused him. The Spanish demanded that Charles become Catholic, which Charles knew would cause war in England, so that negotiations failed. In 1625, however, right before he ascended to the throne and without Parliament's permission, he did marry a Catholic, a French princess whom he met on the trip across Europe.

Partially because of his rejection, England declared war against Spain. Charles levied a major tax to provide money for this war, highly unpopular with the people. Charles disbanded Parliament because it refused to agree to taxation for the war. The King could declare war, but the Parliament had to provide the money to carry out the war. This is similar to the balance of power that exists under the U.S. constitution. The county of Lincolnshire, where our story is located, was particularly rebellious about the payment for the war.

As described in the story, the Earl of Lincoln was summoned to court and thrown into the Tower of London, in 1627, for not paying the tax. Five of those who were similarly imprisoned appealed that it was not legal to hold them without a trial: *habeas corpus*.

146

The Five Knights lost their appeal, but the King was later forced to agree to a bill from Parliament, the Petition of Right, that granted rights including *habeas corpus* to the people. The fact that the King was perceived to be overstepping his legal bounds was a major factor in the civil war that followed in England.

The other factor in the civil war was the religious one. King Charles was, in name, Protestant, but perhaps partly because of his marriage to the French princess, he leaned toward Catholicism. Many Catholic customs were kept at court, Church of England services became more Catholic, and Puritans were increasingly oppressed and increasingly rebellious. They were primarily responsible for England's civil war, which broke out fifteen years after our story. The Massachusetts Puritans did not want civil war, however, and both Mercy's husband and Simon went to England to make sure the King understood their position.

Each of the three religions—Catholic, Protestant Church of England, and Puritan—was intolerant of the others, although individuals, perhaps like Simon Bradstreet, might have held more accepting views. While the Puritans came to the New World to escape persecution in England and for the freedom to worship, they did not grant that freedom to others. They persecuted Quakers, and exiled those who didn't believe as they did. We are so accustomed to thinking that America was founded on principles of religious freedom that it is hard for us to recognize the intolerance of the Puritans.

The Dudley family, as described in the story, was forced to leave England because they would not pay the King's tax for the war, and because they were accused of harboring John Holland, who had circulated incitements to others not to pay the tax.

## Dates

I have tried to be accurate about the sequence of events, but I have taken some liberty with dates. For instance, the Earl was imprisoned in March, not May, 1627. We don't know Anne's actual birthdate, so her age is a guess. Anne is thought to have been fifteen in 1627. Many dates recorded in the period were vague, and two different calendars were in use, each a year apart.

## What Remains

If you visit the town of Boston in Lincolnshire, England, you will find the huge church the Dudley family attended next to the market square, just as in the story. Supposedly Boston got its name from the church, St. Botolph's. Reverend Cotton's cherry pulpit still stands in the center of the church. (The famous American Puritan, Cotton Mather, was named for Reverend Cotton.) Today there are pews throughout the church and the congregation doesn't stand. There is a modern stained glass window in the church, which is an artist's imagined portrait of Anne.

Markets are still held today in the square. Photographs from the nineteenth century show the square so crammed with livestock it would have been impossible to move.

Tattershall Castle also remains much as described in the story. Once fallen into ruin, it has been restored to the magnificence of Anne's time. Its unusual red brick glows in the sun. From the top of the castle one can see the flat ground stretching for miles, with the church in Boston sometimes visible. There are still fens, although most have been drained since the time of the story.

On the mantle of the huge fireplace on the second floor of the castle there is a rabbit with shiny, worn ears among the other stone carvings. There does not now appear to be a secret room, but perhaps it was lost over the years and the renovations.

## To My Dear and Loving Husband

*If ever two were one, then surely we.*
*If ever man were lov'd by wife, then thee.*
*If ever wife was happy in a man,*
*Compare with me, ye women, if you can.*

*I prize thy love more than whole Mines of gold,*
*Or all the riches that the East doth hold.*
*My love is such that Rivers cannot quench,*
*Nor ought but love from thee give recompense.*

*Thy love is such I can in no way repay;*
*The heavens reward thee manifold I pray.*
*Then while we live, in love let's so persever,*
*That when we live no more, we may live ever.*

*— Anne Dudley Bradstreet*

# About the Author

Gretchen Gibbs grew up in a small town in Massachusetts, close to Boston, named for the English Boston near where Anne Dudley lived. She obtained her Ph.D. in clinical psychology from Harvard University, which recently dedicated the Anne Dudley Bradstreet gate in Anne's honor. As a psychologist, Gretchen taught, practiced, and conducted research for many years, and published books and articles in psychology as well as short stories, memoir, and poetry. *Anne of the Fens* is her second novel. *The Book of Maggie Bradstreet* was her first, written about Anne's granddaughter during the 1692 witch trials. Gretchen is descended from both Maggie and Anne.

## *Praise for The Book of Maggie Bradstreet*

"In a world of darkness, of witches and devils and spectral evidence, our eyes catch a glint of light: the wry and indomitable Maggie Bradstreet. As we enter her reality from the inside out, we, like Maggie, wonder if the end of the world is at hand. The novel is a young woman's story, but also the story of anyone who has ever tried to fathom the mysteries of the human heart."

Rebecca McClanahan, author of
*Word Painting* and *The Riddle Song*

"Gretchen Gibbs brings Puritan New England to life. Too gutsy for her own time, Maggie is a girl today's readers will understand. The novel is a page-turner—part mystery, part romance, part coming-of-age story. Struggling against witchcraft hysteria, Maggie is a bewitching heroine."

Mary Makofske, author of *Traction*

"Gretchen Gibbs has written a book so tender and fresh that the voice gets inside your head. Its dark brilliance gives this debut novel the rare quality of making the heroine exist now and also in another time. Maggie Bradstreet pulls you into a very real yet incomprehensible world of spells and fear."

Judy Pedersen, author of *When Night Time Comes Near*

"I was totally absorbed in this novel! The writing absolutely catches the voice of a young girl trying to understand the horrible events around her, and the story itself—even for those of us who know something of the witchcraft trials—was mesmerizing. I was brought to tears at times. The characters were all beautifully developed. It's an ageless story of people believing lies and getting caught up in mass hysteria, relevant as well today."

Donna Spector, author of *The Candle of God*

"The story of the storm of witchcraft accusation that occurred at Andover during the Salem witch trials is insightfully told here by a descendant of the Bradstreets, a respected Massachusetts family whose solid standing in the community was not enough to protect them from a theocracy built upon fear."

Kathy-Ann Becker, author of
*Silencing the Women: The Witch Trials of Mary Bliss Parsons*

"Early American Puritanism was vexed with religious intolerance, ignorance and fear. Maggie Bradstreet is a child who questions her elders and their politics. Her loyal friendships lead her and her readers to hell and back as she witnesses the eerie witch hunts of Andover, Massachusetts. Just when we feel we cannot read on any longer, curiosity gets the best of us and we learn that the most painful part of the story brings an epiphany that restores unity to the small town. Thank God for strong-minded souls like Maggie Bradstreet. And may Tobey's memory be honored forever too! Gretchen Gibbs's research and sensitivity culminate in a stunning novel."

Donna Reis, author of *No Passing Zone* and *Certain*

Made in the USA
San Bernardino, CA
13 November 2015